Bottom of Suez

By Hamilton Teed

(George Heber Hamilton Teed (1886-1938))

First Published by Columbine Publishing Co. Ltd.
London, 1939

Stillwoods Edition 2018

Stillwoods.Blogspot.Ca

Catalogue Information:
Title: Bottom of Suez
Author: Hamilton Teed
(George Heber Hamilton Teed (1886-1938))
First/Previous Edition by: Columbine Publishing Co. Ltd.
This edition: Stillwoods, 2018. (Doug Frizzle)
ISBN Canada: 978-1-988304-54-0
Blog: http://ghteed.blogspot.com/
Storefront: http://www.lulu.com/spotlight/lulubook22

WHAT would happen if the Suez Canal were suddenly destroyed? What would that mean to Britain, to Mussolini—to civilisation?

This is one of the problems which Hamilton Teed sets himself to solve in his amazing mystery story BOTTOM OF SUEZ. The way in which Grant Rushton, prince of sleuths, deals with the problems and the adventures which face him in these extraordinary pages will prove once again that even as Rushton is the prince of detectives, so is Teed the prince of storytellers.

After producing a proof copy of this edition of **Bottom of Suez**, the source of the novel was found to be '**The Great Canal Plot**' first published in the magazine *The Sexton Blake Library*, 2nd Series, No. 19, 31 October 1925. It was subsequently republished again in the library, No. 590 of 1937. The cover image is adapted from that edition. For copyright reasons, the characters had to be renamed for the Columbine hardcover issue.

October 2018.

CHAPTER 1.

In a large, lofty apartment, sumptuously furnished, in the Italian Renaissance period, a woman sat in a richly upholstered inlaid chair, her attitude one of nervous expectation.

A close observer might have fancied there was a tinge of fear in the way her eyes sought the great closed door opposite her from time to time, as well as in the incessant twitching of her fingers about the handle of the short parasol which leant against one knee.

And this appeared incongruous; for in her dress and manner she was decidedly a woman of fashion, and, one would think, of considerable position and authority.

The haughty tilt of her nose and the natural disdain of her shoulders were those fitted to one accustomed to command and not to obey. And yet there is no other word to describe the odd jerkiness of her attitude while she sat waiting.

She had been shown into the room nearly an hour before, and since then not a soul had come near her. In Cairo—for the vast room was in a house in that city, and the time of the year was in the very height of the winter season—in the house of a native prince, it would have been customary for a servant to bring her coffee and a silver dish of sweetmeats; but no such courtesy had been shown her—a significant thing when one considers the customs of the country.

It seemed almost as if this had been deliberately withheld, and that there must be a definite reason for her to be kept waiting as she had been. As a matter of fact, this was exactly the case, and the woman, not being by any means a fool, knew it.

Her wait had just gone an hour, when suddenly, without the slightest warning, the big carved door opposite her opened, and a white-clad servant stood aside to permit the master of the house to enter.

He was a tall Egyptian, whose age was difficult to guess, for the cold dignity of his countenance was topped by a blue silk turban which adorned his head. For the rest, he was dressed in orthodox English morning clothes.

At sight of him the woman rose and made a sort of half-curtsy, to which the man responded with a cold bow. Then he made a sweeping gesture with his hand.

"Be seated, madame," he said in French. Then, as she did so, he drew up a heavy, carved armchair, and followed her example.

It was noticeable that he did not apologise for having kept her waiting.

She obeyed his request—or, rather, command— and sat looking at him. Now she was visibly not so nervous, for her fingers were quiescent, though pressed tight about the handle of her parasol, and her eyes were steadier.

Every particle of her manner seemed to be eager to impress her host favourably, and there were many highly placed men in Cairene society—natives, as well as foreigners—who would have given a good deal to find that same woman so obviously willing to echo their slightest wish as she was to please the dark-skinned man who sat opposite her. But for him he seemed quite unaffected by either her manner or her beauty. And she was beautiful, as anyone will agree who has been in Cairo during the season and has seen the lovely Greek, Madame Goupolis, at the opera, the races, or at Shepheard's.

"Well, madame?"

Again the man spoke; but this time, curiously enough, he spoke in English.

"I am come—to report, prince," she answered, after a pause. "I have been successful."

"We shall discuss to what degree—presently," he answered coldly. "While I was abroad I was informed that the man who was to be removed had been dealt with. But I have also understood that it was more by accident than design. And I think, if you will recall our last conversation, madame, it is not by accident that we look for results."

The woman's eyes flashed. It was only for a moment, and would have boded ill for anyone upon whom she dared to vent her anger at such a cool insult. But with this man, who held her life in the hollow of his hand, she dared not forget herself. Nevertheless, her voice quivered a little as she replied:

"There are those who, as usual, are only too willing to whisper against me. Your Highness should be best able to judge whether what I achieved was by accident or according to set plan. In the past, Prince Menes did not seek to form his opinions from the gossip of underlings."

"Enough of that tone, madame," he replied, coldly. "I form my opinions in a way which is, and always will be, beyond your range of intelligence. Give me your report and I shall judge whether you have done well or ill—whether the sentence once passed against you shall be carried out, or commuted."

At these last words the woman visibly flinched, and her voice held fear in it as she murmured:

"Pardon, your Highness. It is difficult for me to fight against enemies who strike only in the dark. But hear me, I pray you, and then you be my judge as to whether I have done well or no.

"In accordance with instructions, I travelled to the French Riviera and took up quarters in Monte Carlo. There, as you know, I found the man I was seeking—Prince Parvenov, the Russian who had gained my confidence when I believed he was the emissary of a Power that shall be nameless.

"It was not easy to renew association with him, for he was suspicious. Therefore, it was necessary for me to secure the services of a man of daring, who would be willing to do what had to be done for a price. I found such a man, and I was able to offer him a price which was acceptable to him."

"So I have been informed. What was the name of the man?"

"His real name I cannot swear to; but I have been told that it is Hasford—John Hasford. He was known on the Riviera as David Stone, an artist of wealth."

"An Englishman?" And as he spoke the two words, the dark eyes of the man burned with a deep hatred.

"Yes—but a renegade."

"That is for proof, but go on, please."

"I secured the services of this man. He had been for twenty years a prisoner on Devil's Island, the French penal settlement off the coast of South America, and he is a man with many hatreds in his life; for not only was he convicted and sent there for a crime he did not commit, but he had scores to settle with some of those who had been officials at the penal settlement during the time of his incarceration."

"Ah, how could you pay him his price?"

"I could tell him the whereabouts of one of those officials who had retired and whom he could not locate. That was all he asked."

"Well?"

"We laid our plans carefully. I wrote a letter to Prince Parvenov, asking for a last rendezvous, and worded it in such a manner that he could scarcely refuse. I named the place as the summer house in the garden of his villa on the Nice-Monte Carlo road, and this man, David

Stone, accompanied me to the rendezvous. As we expected, a man was sitting inside the summer house. It was, to all appearances, Prince Parvenov. My companion stole across, and, reaching through the open window, wrung his neck as quickly and as noiselessly as he would have twisted the neck of a chicken. Then we got away."

"And discovered that after all a mistake had been made," put in the prince with a slight sneer.

"It was a mistake anyone might make," said the woman, on the defence. "How were we to know that a messenger was coming through from Turkey to see Prince Parvenov? How were we to know that he would be at that particular rendezvous at the moment when Parvenov should have been there? This man who did what I asked is no fool. On the contrary, he is one of the most cold-blooded persons I have ever met, and I have met a few in this country, prince."

"Never mind that," he rejoined curtly. "Let me finish your report for you. To be brief, a mistake was made, and a perfectly unknown individual was killed instead of Parvenov. More than that; as police investigations proceeded, it was found that the man who had been known on the French Riviera as Prince Parvenov, a Russian refugee, was not the real Prince Parvenov at all, but a common impostor, a foster-brother of the real Prince Parvenov, who had betrayed his foster-parents to death in Russia, and who thought he had also betrayed his foster-brother to the same fate. I know all about how the real prince was then found to be a vagabond flower-seller on the Promenade des Anglais in Nice, madame."

"If you know all that, Prince, then you will know that the impostor whom we thought was Prince Parvenov was at last killed, as had been arranged."

"I grant that. Who killed him?"

"The same man—the man whom men call the Black Eagle."

"Ah!"

There was distinct interest in Menes' tone.

"The Black Eagle! I have heard of that man, but I had not connected him with the man you made use of in Monte Carlo."

"It is the same, prince. I should have informed you of this before, but it has not been possible to see you. I could do nothing but wait for your return to Egypt."

Prince Menes shot a swift look at the woman, as if he wanted to make sure whether she was daring to mock him, for his last absence from Egypt was not a thing the arrogant Egyptian was pleased to have mentioned to him.

In his own country, it was for him to command, and there were many thousands who obeyed his slightest whim. It was Menes who was supreme head of the ancient Order of Ra, which, despite the decline in Egypt throughout the centuries, has flourished in secret in the desert, and the cult of which is the same to-day as it was ten thousand years ago.

Those who have followed any of the cases in which the famous criminologist, Grant Rushton, was pitted against the Menes of the present day— the man who was supposed to be a reincarnation of that first Egyptian Pharaoh of old—will know what purpose this man of evil mind had in the world.

They will recall how the beautiful Greek woman, Madame Goupolis, who had been intriguing throughout Egypt and India for years, had become infatuated the previous year in Cairo with the so-called Prince Parvenov; and how, because she had trusted him and had confided to him some of the secrets of the secret order for which she was working, she had been sentenced to death by Menes and the inner council of the order.

She had been given one chance to have this sentence commuted. That was, to carry out the killing of Parvenov; and how that was accomplished is already known.

It is known, too, how Grant Rushton and his assistant, Tony Fairways, took a hand in that game, and not only discovered that the dead Prince Parvenov was a scoundrelly impostor, but also unearthed the real prince and reinstated him in his family fortunes and his good name.

The Black Eagle made a mistake in his first attempt to kill Parvenov, just as Madame Goupolis was confessing to Menes, but he did not fail the second time, and it was none other than Grant Rushton himself who saw that killing—one which by every law, human and divine, was justified.

But what Madame Goupolis did not know was that she was touching on a sore spot when she dwelt on Menes' last journey abroad.

The Egyptian had gone to England with a carefully laid-out plan to secure English girls for the purposes of the temples of Ra in the desert.

Vestals, they were to be called; but Grant Rushton, who foiled that purpose, knew only too well what their fate would have been had Menes succeeded. But even as the ship had lain off the English coast, ready to leave with its human cargo —among whom was none other than Mademoiselle Yvonne Cartier—Rushton and Tony had arrived in the nick of time, and not only had the prisoners been rescued and Menes' plans nipped in the bud, but the Egyptian himself had been turned over to the British authorities.

So, in thinking that she might be daring to mock him about that, Menes was mistaken.

The Greek woman was far too absorbed in her own affairs to dwell on what he had been doing, and too much in fear of the consequences to mock him, even if she had known what had happened.

How Menes had come to be released is one of the mysteries which are never explained. Before he had been brought to trial an order had come through that he was to be deported to his own country without trial, and this had been done.

One could guess that it had some connection with a wider policy, but that is all. At any rate, Menes had been permitted to return to Egypt, and he wasn't back an hour before his deep, scheming, Oriental mind was again busy with plots against the British. For he was of the minority that had opposed any treaty with England.

Menes was the supreme head of the order of Ra, but he was also the guiding spirit of that very modern Egyptian secret society known as the White Flag Society. This society is supposed to be the central organisation of the Egyptian Nationalists; but it is, in reality, nothing but a hot-house and forcing bed for murderous intrigue against the British, and ninety per cent. of the murders in Egypt and the Sudan have their genesis in this organisation.

And it was of this White Flag gang that Madame Goupolis had been an agent for some years—a trusted agent, and well paid. Until she had made that one false step of becoming infatuated with the Russian impostor, and had trusted him with some of the secrets of the order. Little wonder is it, therefore, that she had been in a state of nerves when she had obeyed Menes' summons to attend him at his house that afternoon.

"The Black Eagle."

Again Menes pronounced the name of the mysterious and

ruthless criminal who had emerged from the welter of Devil's Island not long ago, and whom he had not connected with the agent who had acted for Madame Goupolis in the affair at Monte Carlo until that moment. Then suddenly he reached over and touched a small silver bell.

"We shall discuss this matter over some coffee and cigarettes," he said briefly. "If you can interest me it will be to your advantage, madame."

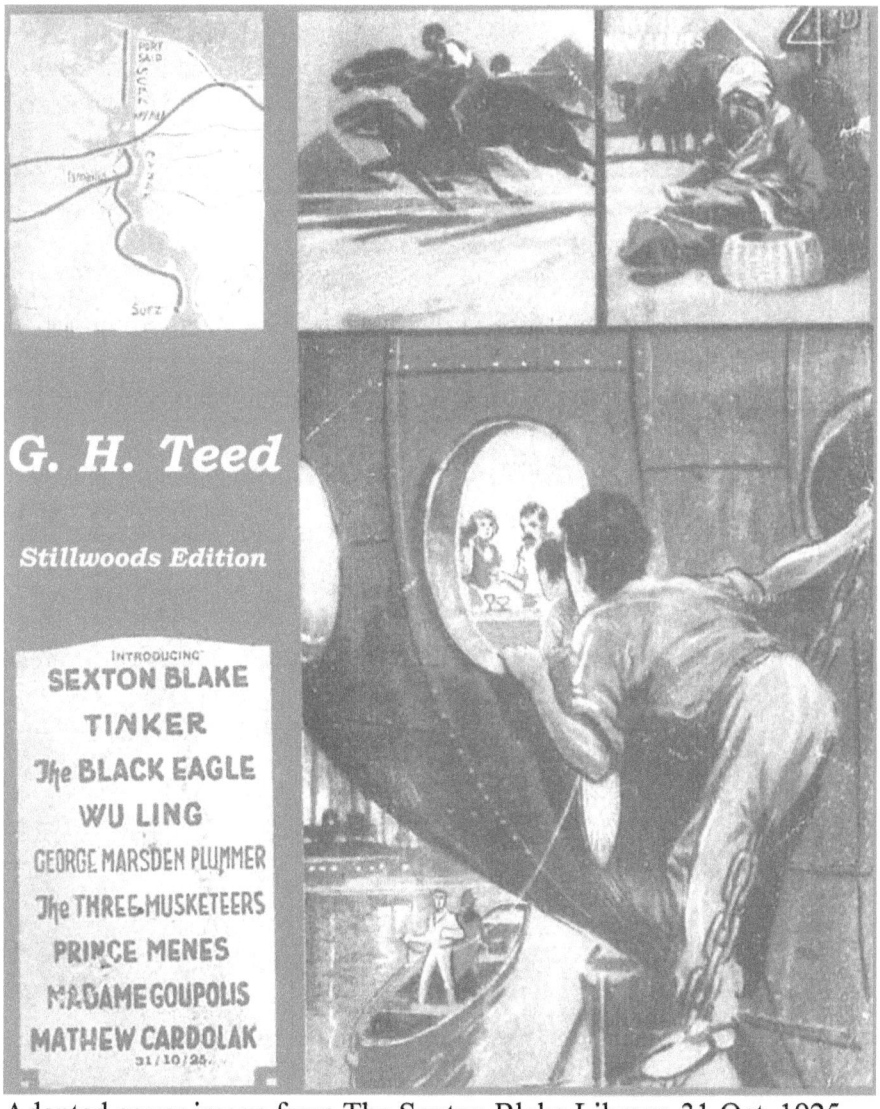

G. H. Teed

Stillwoods Edition

INTRODUCING
SEXTON BLAKE
TINKER
The BLACK EAGLE
WU LING
GEORGE MARSDEN PLUMMER
The THREE MUSKETEERS
PRINCE MENES
MADAME GOUPOLIS
MATHEW CARDOLAK
31/10/25.

Adapted cover image from The Sexton Blake Library, 31 Oct, 1925.

CHAPTER 2.

A Nubian servant served the coffee and cigarettes on a large silver tray, and when he had retired Prince Menes attended to the wants of his guest. Then:

"And now, madame, if you please."

Madame Goupolis was a shrewd woman, and she was quick to notice the slight, almost imperceptible change in Menes' tone. It was not yet by any means friendly; but it was, she thought, a trifle less cold than it had been, and she was quick to take the first sign of the advantage it seemed to offer.

No one knew better than she that it was up to her to get Menes really interested if she wished to become reinstated in his confidence.

If she failed she knew that some dark night would find her pretty neck wrung just as effectually as the Black Eagle had wrung that of the man on the Riviera. And she wanted nothing so much as to live and enjoy the sweets of life.

But she had not been slow, had Madame Goupolis, since she had been in Monte Carlo, and for days she had eagerly awaited the return of the prince to Cairo. In her head there had formed a scheme which the prince himself could not have exceeded for daring, and it was this with which she had come to bargain.

"You know what happened in Monte Carlo, prince," she said slowly. "On the successful completion of that affair I returned to Cairo."

"With the assistance of the Monaco authorities," he put in.

"That is so; but still free to continue my work," she said. And Menes, remembering how he had left England a couple of weeks before, did not press the subject. "In Cairo I again met the man who had helped me in Monte Carlo—the man I shall call the Black Eagle."

"Ah! Is he still here?"

"Yes."

"Did he find the man he was seeking?"

"Yes."

"What happened?"

"What he intended. He wrung his neck—just like that." And as she spoke the word Madame Goupolis made a gesture with her right hand from one side to the other.

"What was the name of that man?" persisted Menus.

"Poiret—Jean Poiret."

"I shall probably be able to get a report on the matter through my secretary. Did the authorities do anything?"

"I believe not, prince. There was a formal inquiry—that is all. So, as I have said, I again met the Black Eagle here. He had accomplished his purpose, and he was not indisposed to philander. I cultivated him—with a purpose."

"That is what I am waiting for, madame. What was that purpose?"

"To please you, prince—to regain the position in your confidence which I have lost—to rid myself from the obnoxious attentions of the spies who follow me day and night—for many reasons. And I think I have succeeded. Listen, prince. Have you ever heard of one Mathew Cardolak, a very wealthy American multi-millionaire, who intrigues continually in the Near East?"

"You will ask me next if I know myself," he responded. "I know Mathew Cardolak intimately. What of him, madame?"

"If you know him you will perhaps know of three persons whom he sometimes employs to carry out his purposes. Like the man they call the Black Eagle, they are renegade Englishmen. I know what they are regarding France, and I know that he would do anything— anything to hurt the French Nation, and the French people. And in this way three persons who act for Mathew Cardolak will join in any plans which have for their aim the injuring of the country they hate. They are called the Three Musketeers."

"I can tell you more than that about the Three Musketeers," put in the prince dryly. "I could tell you that on more than one occasion they have sought sanctuary in Egypt, and have received it from the White Flag Society—but go on."

"The Three Musketeers have been in the Mediterranean on the big steam yacht Sultan, which belongs to Mathew Cardolak. I met one of them —the one whose name is Pherison—here in Cairo. I had a talk with him and I think I can say that he will do what I asked. I will tell you what that was presently.

"Following that, prince, I discovered that there is, hiding here in Cairo, a man who has been waiting for your return to Egypt. He is a man of great power and you know him well. He is most anxious to see you—or was—but I have seen him, and talked with him, and he, too, has agreed to a suggestion which I made to him."

"You are beginning to interest me, madame. What else? What is the name of this person?"

"Prince Wu Ling, the man who holds China in the hollow of his hand."

"Prince Wu Ling, here in Cairo."

Menes was obviously stirred by this news.

"But I do not understand that," he went on. "I have had before me since my return, a list containing the names of all foreigners staying in Cairo at present. I do not see the name of Wu Ling on that list?"

"Nor would you for he is in close hiding."

"And he came here to see me?"

"Yes, prince."

"If he came here in secret and has remained here for my return, he must have something of value to say," muttered Menes. Then he made a gesture for the woman to continue. And she hadn't played all her cards yet, for now she bent forward a little, her manner considerably more confident than it had been.

"One more person of whom I would speak, prince," she said slowly. "There is a man who has been a fugitive criminal from nearly every country on the globe, but who is still free. He is a man who stops at nothing, and for some eight years now he has been right-hand man to Abdel Krim. This man's name is Brady, and he was at one time a trusted official of the great English police bureau—Scotland Yard. He knows the inside of that system and he can be valuable. Him, too, I have seen."

"With what result?"

"The same as the others. He has agreed to a certain proposal which I made to him."

"And what was this proposal which you made to these people, madame?"

"One which I hope will please you, prince, and one which can only be proceeded with, provided you take the leading part. It is this:

"Mathew Cardolak is on his yacht, the Sultan, which is, at present, lying off Alexandria. Mr. Pherison has returned to the yacht, and, if he keeps his word, will pass on my proposal to Mathew Cardolak. You—you know so much about that man, will know whether he is likely to throw his weight into your side of the scales or not."

"It is true that he is the son of a Mohammedan father and a Jewish mother," remarked Menes thoughtfully. "But even to me, who have followed his movements for years, he is a good deal of a mystery. No one knows what is going on inside that brain of Mathew Cardolak's. Sometimes I have felt sure that he was plotting against the Jews, and that at heart he is a true Mohammedan. It is said that he hates the Jews. And then again, when he has had it in his power to do them great injury, he has held his hand. But until I know what proposals you have made, I cannot give an opinion. And then you are not forgetting that Cardolak is a man of enormous wealth? I think it is safe to place him amongst the three richest men in the world. What can we offer to induce him to join us?"

"Probably no other living person could offer him what you can offer, prince."

"What do you mean, madame?"

"Above all things in life, Mathew Cardolak craves rare antiques. He has spent literally millions on his collection, and he cares not by what means he gets them, and who can offer him such a rich field as you? At a word you could see that none of the treasures come from the newly discovered tombs. That is what I mean. You can offer plenty of difficulties, and can arrange for Cardolak to get the pick of what he wants. Or again, there are still other tombs, the whereabouts of which are unknown to anyone but you who hold the secret Book of the Dead. That is what I mean. You can offer Mathew Cardolak that which money could not buy, and yet what he would rather have than anything else in the world."

"By Allah! But you have said it!" exclaimed Menes. "That never before occurred to me, and I confess it. Cardolak never entered into my scheme of things. Go on, madame."

"Pherison has promised to speak to him. And the others are agreed. So it rests with you, prince, whether my plan is proceeded with, and that plan is this:

"It is our aim, the aim of the White Flag Society, to smash the power of Britain in Egypt and in India. To that end, every human unit in the society is dedicating his life, and there are thousands waiting to fill their places when they are gone. But we must strike outside Egypt as well as within its borders. We must harry the British at every point, and in every way possible. Therefore it has occurred to me that men such as I have named, those three renegades who call themselves the Three Musketeers; the man who is known as the Black Eagle; the renegade police officer, Flash Brady; and by no means least, the wealthy and powerful Chinese prince, Wu Ling, would make a strong, ruthless and effective combination if they could be brought under one control.

"Prince Wu Ling does not need money. He is rich and as powerful as an emperor. But he will help us at this side of the world, if we help him in the Far East. In this case it is an alliance. The man Brady will do anything for money, prince, if it be large enough. The Three Musketeers will do anything that Cardolak says, for they are his agents—in his pay and under his protection. The Black Eagle, I am less certain about him. He does not need money, but he has hinted that he is the enemy of all mankind, so that I think he will come in. And for Cardolak—I have already said what his price would be.

"So now it rests with you. I have arranged to communicate myself with the others as soon as I have your answer. I took so much upon myself that I have even made all arrangements for a joint meeting—if you agree. A telegram will settle it. What is your answer, prince?"

"A meeting. Where?"

"A secret meeting on board Mathew Cardolak's yacht."

"When?"

"To-morrow night if you can arrange it."

"There would need to be safeguards," muttered Menes. "There would be the danger of betrayal."

"I have thought of that," said the woman, coolly. "At all times we could have a safe leavening of our own people, and if there were any signs of betrayal it could be dealt with quickly enough."

"But each one of these men is a criminal of experience," he went on. "If jealousies arose—if there was a dispute as to leadership . . ."

"That must at all times be in your hands or in the control of the deputy you should appoint," she put in. "In some cases it might be wiser to give the control for the time being to one or another. That would depend entirely on circumstances. And always your word must be supreme."

"If they could be kept under control it is a great plan," he rejoined. "I give you credit for that, madame. And in any event no harm can be done by getting them together and discussing matters. So I agree. Make your arrangements for to-morrow night, madame, I shall motor through to Alexandria during the morning if I hear from you that all is well. The others will have to make their own arrangements for getting there, and no comment must be aroused. See that they are circumspect."

And at those words Madame Goupolis heaved an inward sigh of relief, for she knew that she had achieved the first part of her purpose, and she had enough confidence in her own brain to believe that she would gain the rest.

CHAPTER 3.

It was nearly six o'clock in the evening before Madame Goupolis left Prince Menes' palace, which stood on the outskirts of the fashionable foreign quarter of Cairo.

The prince himself saw her to her limousine— a marked change from the manner in which she had been received on her arrival.

It would soon be time to dress for dinner, but the Greek woman did not drive directly back to Shepheard's.

Instead she gave her man an address in a poor part of the native quarter, close to the bazaar. Apparently she knew all about the section, for before arriving there she took care to draw a heavy black veil well over her features.

When the car stopped, she got out and went along on foot until she came to a small curio shop, which she entered.

An ancient, bearded Arab was the only person to be seen, and as she approached the counter she uttered a single word in Arabic.

He made no answer, but, turning, went to the back of the shop, where he disappeared behind some rugs which hung from a rafter, almost reaching the floor.

The woman followed him, and waited there while he opened a panel in the wall.

There was a narrow flight of stairs to be seen, lighted by a single oil-lamp. The old man stood aside for her to enter, and as soon as she was within he closed the panel after her.

She went up some twenty steps or so until she came to a very narrow landing above. Facing this was a closed door, on which she tapped lightly.

Nothing happened for a few moments, but then there came a shuffling sound from within, and the door opened. Only a hand was visible holding the door, but the Greek woman stepped inside with an air of knowing what she was doing, and the door closed after her.

She was now in a small but extremely well-furnished room, which was illuminated by a big lamp in a swinging copper brazier from the centre of the ceiling.

But Madame Goupolis had no eyes for surroundings which were familiar to her. She turned at once to face the person who stood behind the door, and as she did so she raised her veil.

The other bowed gravely, and made a gesture that she should be seated. She swept to a chair, her manner much more confident than it

14

had been in the house of the Egyptian, and looked up at the tall Celestial who stood awaiting her pleasure.

Neither of them seemed to find it an incongruous thing that a high-caste Chinaman should be occupying that hidden room in the heart of the Cairo bazaar.

And yet it was none other than the notorious Prince Wu Ling, supreme head of the Brotherhood of the Yellow Beetle, and more powerful, in a way, than Menes himself.

"I have seen him," announced the woman. "He is pleased to know you are in Cairo, but I could not enlighten him as to why you had come."

Again Wu Ling bowed gravely.

"That is only for the ears of Prince Menes," he said coldly. "Did you speak to him of the other matter, madame?"

"Yes."

"And his answer is?"

"He wants to know more. He thinks the arrangement for holding a meeting on the yacht is excellent, and suggests to-morrow night as convenient. He hopes that will suit you as well, prince, but regrets it would not be good policy for him to ask you to accompany him when he leaves Cairo. He thinks the whole thing should be done as secretly as possible."

"That is wise," rejoined the Chinaman tonelessly. "The place and time are suitable to me, madame. I am obliged to you for the trouble you have taken. If you are communicating with his Highness again I shall be grateful if you will inform him that I shall be there."

"Then that is all, and I shall go along," remarked Madame Goupolis, rising. "I have others to see to-night."

"One moment, madame, I beg you," said Wu Ling, lifting his hand.

Then he clapped his palms together, and almost at once a heavy rug at one side of the room was pushed aside, and a stout, elderly Celestial entered.

If Grant Rushton had been there he would have recognised this individual as San, Wu Ling's right-hand man, and the one living person of whom he made anything like a confidant. San it was who had been Wu Ling's tutor when the Prince had been a child, and San it was who had followed his master like a faithful dog through all the years that had followed.

Madame Goupolis was a clever woman, and she was pluming herself that she had managed things very nicely. But she had not the faintest conception of the calibre of the tall, grave-faced Chinaman who was aeons removed from her in subtlety.

San was holding a small velvet cushion on which reposed a velvet case such as one receives from jewellers. He carried this across until he stood in front of the Greek woman, and, stepping forward, Wu Ling pressed the catch.

Madame Goupolis, slightly puzzled, was watching his actions, and as the cover flew up, revealing the contents of the case, she gave a gasp of sheer admiration.

And well she might. She had been the recipient of many beautiful jewels in her time, but never in all her life had she gazed upon two more perfect pearls that lay like two great pale pink drops against the white silk of the lining. They were worth almost anything in the Rue de la Paix, and she knew it. And one glance at the impassive face of the Chinaman told her he was offering them to her.

She hesitated; then Wu Ling took the case and laid it in her hands.

"For you, madame," he said, suavely. "They are unworthy of your lovely skin, but I beg you to accept the gift as a slight acknowledgment of what you have done for me."

"But I have really done very little, Prince Wu Ling," she stammered, and when Goupolis stammered she needed to be really deeply affected. "I—I . . ."

"You will please me," urged the voice of the Celestial as he pressed the case upon her, and, as if in a dream, she took them. Then, almost before she knew it, she was out on the landing again, and the door was closed after her.

Nor did she see Wu Ling return to San when she was gone and shrug as he said:

"She is unworthy of two such gems, San, even if they are such a trifle. She is clever for one of the West, and she may prove useful. She does not dream that I know all about her recent difficulties with Prince Menes. It is as well that she should continue to think as she does. No one can tell what will be the outcome of all this business, and it may be useful to know where we have her at the start. And forget not, San, that while it suits our purpose, we are as children. We listen and we agree. And then we shall see what we shall see."

Upon which Wu Ling allowed himself one of his rare smiles and San, after a low bow, withdrew, chuckling fatly to himself as the rug curtain hid him from the august person of his master.

On reaching the bottom of the staircase, Madame Goupolis tapped lightly on the panel, which was opened a few moments later by the old curio dealer. He made no remark, but stood aside for her to pass out.

Indeed, it was no new thing for the secret room above to be used, for he was a humble member of the White Flag Society, and above his shop was that secret chamber, just as there were scores and scores of other secret chambers for the use of the White Flag gang throughout the whole of Cairo.

From the shop of the curio dealer Madame Goupolis drove back to Shepheard's. She dismissed the car in front, telling the man she would not require him again that evening.

She stopped in the lounge to get her key and some letters, and then she ascended at once to her rooms, for it was time to dress for dinner.

She took particular care with her toilet that evening. Not that she did not always give her maid an exacting time of it, but on this occasion she was more finicky than usual.

While her maid arranged her hair she took the jewel-case which she had received from Wu Ling and opened it on her lap.

She took out the two great pearls and examined them more closely, and her eyes glistened with delight as she saw that they were even more beautiful than she had thought. They had been set as drop ear-rings, and she suddenly made up her mind that she would wear them that evening.

So she chose a silver lamé dress to set them off, and for the only other jewellery threw two ropes of pearls about her neck and slipped a single great pearl and diamond ring on her finger.

When she finally descended she was easily the most beautiful and perfectly dressed woman in the place—and she knew it.

Nor did it matter one whit to her that there were those who whispered "white devil" to themselves as she passed. While she was in favour with Prince Menes they dare not voice those words aloud.

She was not dining alone. In the lounge a man was waiting for her, and as she appeared he rose. She came towards him with a dazzling smile which would have "rattled" a good many men. But this person merely bowed, allowing his eyes to rest on her approvingly, the while his lips muttered some compliments which were pleasing to her.

But David Stone, as he was known at Shepheard's, was as little affected by the sensuous, exotic appeal of the woman as the Sphinx itself would have been.

It pleased him that his companion was beautiful and worth looking at, but beyond that his criticism did not go.

He knew too well what sort of a mind was behind that lovely shell, and then, to, he and the woman shared a secret which made their relationship a peculiar one.

They passed into the restaurant leisurely, and the head waiter hurried forward to conduct them to the table which the Black Eagle had chosen.

He had already taken care to order a dinner which he knew would appeal to her, so they were able from the start to converse.

They filled in a few minutes in discussing the choice of wines, and then, as the orchestra began, the woman turned and gazed about the restaurant, apparently oblivious of the battery of eyes directed in her direction—eyes that were filled with every conceivable expression—from the awed wonder of the young girl abroad for the first time, the envy and malice of the more sophisticated women, the bold admiration of a certain type of man, and the dumb worship of half a dozen young calves, to the doddering leer of the old "dogs" who thought they knew all about her.

But not one of those glances was as quietly cynical as that of the Black Eagle as he surveyed them.

And then suddenly Madame Goupolis turned to him, her forehead slightly puckered with a frown.

"Please look at that table over in the alcove, my friend," she said, as she curled her fingers round the slim stem of a cocktail glass and sipped the contents. "The one with the party of young people. They look English."

"Yes—I see them, madame," he answered, after glancing across the room. "What of them?"

"Do you see the young fellow with his arm in a black silk sling? His face is very white—he looks ill, and I have heard him coughing. His face, somehow, is familiar to me, and yet I cannot remember just where I have seen him before. But it seems to recall something of an unpleasant nature."

The Black Eagle finished his cocktail and waited until the waiter had served the oysters. Then when the man was gone he glanced at her and smiled slightly.

"You are not mistaken, madame," he said. "You have seen that young man before and it is quite possible that the recollection is not exactly pleasant. He does look ill, and as you say he has a painful-sounding cough. In fact, I saw him about the hotel during the afternoon, and, from what I overheard said among the friends he is with, it would seem that he has been the victim of a serious accident, in which several limbs were broken and his lungs punctured by one of his ribs. He was ordered to Egypt, I gathered, in the hope that the dry air would benefit his lungs."

"All of which is quite interesting, I daresay," she remarked, a little impatiently, when he paused. "But I do not yet recall where I have seen him before, and why a young man like that should give me an unpleasant feeling."

"Perhaps I can tell you why," said the Black Eagle. "You saw that young man last in Monte Carlo, at a time which you are scarcely likely to forget. And he was associated with a person for whom you entertain a most lively dislike, I believe."

"You are very mysterious, monsieur," she responded. "And tell me, pray, who is this young man?"

"He is—or was—assistant to the London criminologist, Grant Rushton," answered the Black Eagle, as he turned to his oysters.

CHAPTER 4.

On moonlight nights, in the season in Cairo, it is the correct thing after dinner for the guests at the big hotels in the town to drive along the Meni House Road as far as the Great Pyramid and back again.

Sometimes one goes on to Meni House Hotel or the great Heliopolis Hotel for a dance; but the lazy are content to sit for a while and dream in the shadow of those vast monuments which the vanity of kings reared in a bygone day, and let the atmosphere of the desert night sink in.

There is something about the pyramids and the sphinx in the moonlight that strips the tawdry tinsel away from the pleasure-loving present, no matter how frivolously inclined one may be.

And be sure on those nights, the beggars which are always an infernal nuisance there, as in other parts of Egypt, are more of a pest than ever. Like ghouls of the desert they gather in their rags and their filth and make the lovely nights hideous with their whines and curses and quarrellings.

Nor was it destined to be any different on the night when Madame Goupolis dined with the Black Eagle, and when her curiosity was aroused at the sight of a young man whom she could not for the moment recall. Nor is it to be wondered at; for the young fellow who had just arrived at Shepheard's was very different in appearance from the robust person who had been with Grant Rushton at Monte Carlo.

Now, he looked terribly ill. Aside from his left arm, which he carried in a sling, and which told its own tale of some sort of accident, he was chalky white, and his features had the haggard, drawn look of the person who suffers from lung trouble.

In addition, he had a most sepulchral cough which brought a look of pity into the eyes of those who heard him, and it seemed that he was too far gone in the grip of the dread disease for even the dry, healing air of Egypt to avail.

But after the explanation given by the Black Eagle, the Greek woman paid no more attention to the lad.

Her curiosity had been satisfied, and she paused only long enough to think with satisfaction that the curses which she had hurled at the head of Grant Rushton and his assistant were beginning to have effect, before turning to another subject of conversation.

And just about that time the foul nightbirds of the desert were beginning to gather at the Pyramids in anticipation of the harvest which evening should bring forth.

In fact, they had been hanging about the place all day, harrying any parties of tourists who appeared, and, as soon as the victims had departed, quarrelling and snarling over the proceeds like so many carrion.

They had a sort of unwritten law among them regarding "pitches," which it was the first care of each to break whenever it suited his purpose, and, for that reason, most of them travelled in little groups of anything from three or four up to a score.

This was a measure of defence against the others, and it was only the most morose or daring who played a lone hand. But a few there were who worked the game alone, and of these there was one who had not taken up his stand at the Pyramids, except of late.

This individual was an old desert rat whose rags were more filthy, if such a thing were possible, than those of any of the others. He was bent and stooped, and was a most savage, profane old wretch altogether.

When he had first made his appearance a few days previously, some of the others had tried to drive him off, first by jeers, then, when he ignored that form of pleasantry, by threats, and, finally, by direct action.

This latter took the form of a combined attack by some twenty of them, but when they had been met by a furious storm of anger, such as they had never seen before, and when this had been followed up by a rain of horned toads which the old man had jerked from a covered basket and hurled into their faces, they had drawn off, and, like the rats they were, left him in peace.

He had chosen a spot at one corner of one of the smaller of the three pyramids, where he arrived early in the evening, and where he remained until late in the night.

It was by no means as lucrative a spot as he might have found closer to the Great Pyramid.

It was quieter, and fewer tourists passed that way. But, taken all in all, he did not do so badly, and perhaps the alms he received amounted to more than would otherwise have come his way, for the reason that he was not accompanied by a mob that made life unbearable for the tourist who would linger.

The old man made his plea. If he was given charity he called down the blessings of Allah upon the head of him who gave; if he was refused he called down the blessings of Allah just the same, and, more often than not, he who had refused changed his mind out of sheer amazement that he had not cursed.

For the rest, the filthy old beggar kept to himself, eating his evening meal of kous-kous and dates and solitude.

On this particular evening he had taken up his pitch a little after four o'clock, for it was always possible that there would be tourists about after the hour of tea.

In fact, he had not done badly, and when the hour came which meant that those who lived in the big, sumptuous hotels, and brought such wealth to the country, would be taking the evening meal, the old beggar retired into the shadow at the base of the pyramid, and seated himself on the sand.

In the east a full moon was just coming up above the edge of the desert. Through the quivering, magnifying film of the heat, which was still rising from the sand, it looked enormous, almost blood-red, and seemingly so close one could almost touch it.

The evening would be chilly later, but with that moon there would be plenty of visitors along, and the pickings would be good indeed.

Perhaps this was what the solitary old beggar was thinking of as he withdrew into the shadow and squatted down at the base of the lowest "course," which was rough and broken where some vandal of bygone days had carted away the stone for building purposes.

Had there been anyone near just then—which there wasn't—they might have heard the chink of metal as he counted his day's takings, and then a throaty chuckle of satisfaction as he made the total quite a respectable sum. He tucked the coins carefully away inside his dirty rags, and then undid a cloth which he had brought along with him.

From somewhere inside this he took out a handful of dates, a hard kous-kous cake and a flask of water. Then he proceeded to take his evening meal, and for the next ten minutes or so no other sound could be heard in his immediate vicinity but the champ, champ, champ of his teeth and lips as he ate.

When he had quite finished the unpalatable food he drank deep of the flask, which he returned to the interior of the bundle of rags. This he re-tied with some care, after which he drew towards him the basket in which he had brought the horned toads the first day, and which the other beggars still believed to contain a supply of those devilish reptiles.

Now he stood up, and, walking to the corner of the pyramid, stood looking towards the low dip which lies between the two small pyramids and the Great Pyramid.

It is only recently that proper excavations have been made there, and that there has been brought to light the fact that in the hollow lies the sacred funeral boat ditch of the two queens of the great Pharaoh who built the Pyramids.

Old Khufa apparently did not neglect a single detail in order to make quite sure that he and his favourite wives and all his household goods and chattels should be safely ferried across the river to the paradise which was awaiting him.

Down there, too, the workers had recently come upon two small temples which had some bearing upon the two smaller pyramids, and in one of these temples the old beggar knew that certain young men from Cairo gathered each evening; but for what purpose he could not tell.

During the off season those same young natives would gather on one of the lower courses of the Great Pyramid; but now there were too many tourists about for the privacy which they seemed to desire, and, while they hated the visitors with a ferocity that would have appalled the latter could they but have sensed it, they gave way for the time being.

Their day was coming—so they thought—when Egypt would be theirs, and all foreigners swept out of it, or the British, at any rate.

Needless to say, they were the brainless student class, and that small temple was but one of the many places where they made it a practice to gather and plot against the race which has lifted them out of the gutter and made it possible for them to do as they are doing.

With his basket on one arm, and his dirty rag bundle under the other, the old beggar hobbled along towards the spot where the excavations were taking place.

There were some watchmen at one end of the hollows, but they were more than two hundred yards away from the two small temples, and paid no attention to the desert rat.

He approached the temple where the youths from Cairo made it a practice to meet, and then a watcher might have seen him once more swallowed up in the shadow.

He had not entered the temple, however. He had paused outside the tunnel which led to it, and there he squatted down on a loose heap of sand which had been thrown up by the diggers. He laid his rag bundle aside and put his basket between his knees.

He opened the cover, and instead of taking out horned toads, he brought out something which seemed to possess some weight and which for one brief moment seemed to gleam dully in the reflected moonlight from the sand beyond the shadow.

He laid this aside, and thrust his hand into the basket again. This time he brought out a large coil of dark stuff which he proceeded to unwind slowly and carefully.

He worked away for ten minutes or so, until he seemed satisfied that he had unwound enough.

Next he again picked up the first object he had brought forth, and fumbled for a few minutes until he had connected up the end of the cord he had unwound with a knob of the former. He laid it down again, and began to scoop away the sand with his hands.

He made a hole some twelve inches long by six or seven wide and five or six inches deep, and into this he placed the round object to which he had attached the cord.

Then he pushed the sand back over it until the surface of the round object was practically level with the edges of the hole, and over this he scattered just enough sand to keep it concealed from view.

That done, he began moving away from the spot on his haunches, travelling very slowly indeed, and, had anyone been observing him closely they would have seen that he went on scooping out a shallow groove in the sand into which he fed the cord, afterwards pressing the sand back over it.

It took a considerable time to cover the hundred and fifty yards or so between the temple and the corner of the pyramid which he had made his stamping ground; but he managed it at last, and when he was once more in the shadow, he held in his hand one end of a cord which he stretched, concealed in its little tunnel of sand, clear back to the temple where the round metal object had been buried, and it was in contact with that.

He squatted again in the shadow by the lower course of the pyramid, and again drew the basket between his bent knees. From it he took what looked like a small black box, and to this he now attached the free end of the cord which emerged from the sand at his feet.

Next he scooped another hole, into which he placed the black box, and into this he scattered sand, until all but the top was covered. Over the top he dropped just enough to make a film, as it were; and then, like any desert rat, he laid himself down and curled up for a sleep.

Within a radius of a quarter of a mile from him there were more than a hundred beggars, and as many more natives, whose affairs brought them into that vicinity; but not a single one knew that the old beggar who had held his own so well was lying with one ear pressed down over a highly sensitive microphone attachment which was connected up with another microphone a hundred and fifty yards away, that this in turn was made more effective by a "crimped" amplifier which was placed so that it must catch every single word that was uttered in the temple there and carry it along to the base of the course where the dirty old beggar lay as if asleep.

Nor could they have guessed, even if they had known this, that it had only been placed as it was now after the old desert rat had made a highly scientific study of the acoustic properties of the temple—a curious form of knowledge for such a filthy ghoul of the night to possess.

CHAPTER 5.

The beggar had been lying curled up on the sand at the foot of the lowest course of the pyramid for a good half-an-hour or more before anyone came in his direction.

Then a figure appeared, coming from the direction of the Meni House Gate. It was a native, clad somewhat after the Bedouin fashion, with a white cotton cloth covering his lower limbs, and a voluminous cotton burnous about the upper part of his body. The burnous had been drawn over his head, but there was nothing remarkable in that, for it was the general custom of the country after sunset.

He passed the apparently sleeping beggar only a few yards distant, and kept on until he reached the small temple beyond, into which he disappeared. Almost at once three more figures appeared, coming from the same direction, and, they too, made their way to the small temple in question.

Then another showed up, walking alone, and almost immediately after a couple, and then three more. The whole crowd entered the temple, and no one else appeared.

Still the old desert rat lay just as he had been; but now as a voice, clear and distinct, came to him along the buried wire which was connected up with the crimped receiver which he had buried just outside the temple, he raised his head the veriest trifle in order to remove the pressure from his outer ear and thus leave the passage as free as possible to the inner ear. Then he lay motionless, not missing a single word that was being uttered.

The voice was enunciating in Egyptian Arabic, which was familiar enough to the listener, and although the tones were lowered to a key that was not supposed to allow them to carry beyond the immediate circle of listeners, the microphone had been arranged so cunningly that the beggar might just as well have been inside the temple. And what he overheard was something as follows:

"The chief is back, and we shall get into action once more," the voice had begun by saying. "It is but two hours since I have seen him, and he has great plans."

"Which he did not confide in you," broke in a fresh voice in a sneering tone.

"The great one confides in none, as well you know," rejoined the first speaker in an unruffled voice. "But one is permitted to guess, and I know that the first stroke will be made to-morrow."

"To-morrow—are you sure?" put in a new voice.

"I am certain. It is for that you have been summoned to meet here to-night."

"For what purpose?"

"We are to draw lots to see who will carry out what has to be done," was the answer. "It is a great thing, and will bring much glory to the cause."

"What is it?" persisted the other speaker; and just then, out against the pyramid, the huddled bundle of rags might have been seen to move ever so little.

"You will know that presently," rejoined the first speaker. "The draw must take place, and then I shall tell you. It is by the direct orders of the chief, so there must be no delay in carrying it out."

"If it is like the last, it means death to those who are chosen," remarked one whose voice was new to the listener at the other end of the wire. "Since that last affair the cursed infidels (the British) have been more watchful than ever; and it is only two days since they caught two of our brothers who were on the point of getting across the Egyptian border into Tripoli."

(The listener knew the speaker was referring to an abominable murder of a few weeks before, and, although he did not know it, two of the vile assassins, students—as were those in the temple at that moment—had been caught by the police just as they were about to slip across the Egyptian border into Tripoli.)

"And it means death if the orders of the chief are not carried out," was the response of the first speaker, who seemed to be some sort of a petty leader in the White Flag gang. "Orders are orders, and we shall now make the draw. I have brought along the ebony box and the strips of ivory. Four are to carry out what is to be done, and those drawing the four longest strips of ivory will be those to whom the honour falls. In order that none may suspect that all is not fair, I, as usual, will refrain from drawing."

A low murmur seemed now to reach the ears of the listener, and it was not difficult for him to guess that the others were not altogether in agreement that the leader should not take the same risk of drawing which they must take.

But evidently their protests did not go beyond that, for the reason that they were too much in fear of the society to which they belonged, and then, too, the fools were so filled with a fanatical hatred of the

British that they were easily persuaded that it was a matter of supreme honour to be chosen to carry out one of the murders which the plotters were planning.

There were a few faint sounds after the drawing began, and now and then a low voice said something as a strip of ivory was drawn. The listener had to picture what was going on, but a little later knew that he had visualised things with correctness, for again the voice of the leader could be heard:

"The four longest—each man hold up his strip of ivory—that is right. Ah, by Allah. The honour goes to Hassan ib Hassan for the first; to Abdul el Karn for the second; to the brother of Hassan ib Hassan for the third and to Ferin al Fahmy for the fourth. My congratulations, brothers. Now draw close, and you shall hear what has to be done."

And at this point the old beggar by the pyramid again shifted his position a little.

For ten minutes or so the leader talked to the group in the temple.

He went into considerable detail as to what the movements of a certain British official would be on the morrow; and there must have been an efficient spy in the office of that official, for he had his whole programme for the day mapped out from early morning until a certain time in the afternoon, when he should pass a named corner in the bazaar on his way to the British Residency.

And it was at that corner that the projected outrage was to take place.

When he had finished, he laid out the exact instructions which the four assassins were to follow, and then he told them what provision had been made for their escape as soon as the deed was done.

There was some discussion about the latter when he had finished, but eventually the four fools expressed themselves as satisfied, and prepared to carry out their orders to the letter.

That closed that part of the proceedings, and after a short silence the first speaker began a long and fanatical discourse which had obviously been prepared for him by someone much higher up in the White Flag Society, in which he whipped his listeners to a white heat of fanatical passion as he railed against the British and the imagined wrongs which they had inflicted upon Egypt.

It was a disgusting tirade of vicious vituperation, built on lies by a mind that had weltered in the gutter; but it had served its purpose none the less, and by the time he brought it to a close the wire from the microphone was quivering with the chorus of "hos and has" which came along it.

Another silence, and then the petty leader spoke again:

"And now, comrades, I shall prove to you that big things are afoot. You all know that the Goupolis is back in Cairo, and that she has been waiting here for the Great One to return. She visited him at his palace this afternoon. When she arrived she was kept waiting for some time, and no coffee or sweetmeats were served to her.

"But when that Great One had talked with her for a while coffee and cigarettes were served, and when she departed the Great One himself saw her into her car. That is proof that she has again regained his confidence, and from a source, which I need not mention, I know what the proposals are which she made to the chief.

"The Great One has looked favourably upon them, and to-morrow he leaves Cairo."

"Leaves Cairo," exclaimed one of the others. "Is he then leaving Cairo on the day when we are to carry out this new affair?"

"And why not?" asked the first speaker, coldly. "Is it necessary for the Great One to be in the City when a mere detail of the work is being done? And is it not better that he should be miles away at the time, so that the infidels—may Allah cause their tongues to drop out and their eyes to wither from their sockets!—may not be able to connect him with it? We are but humble instruments whom Allah has favoured in permitting us to carry out the plans of the Great One."

"True," murmured several voices, and the old beggar had little difficulty in guessing that the voices were those of the number who had not been "honoured" by drawing one of the four longest strips of ivory.

"Where does he go?" asked another.

"That is part of the new plan which the Goupolis has proposed," answered the first speaker. "I can tell you no more now except that he goes to Alexandria, and that a meeting will be held there. For important purposes it is possible that certain infidels will be admitted as temporary members of the society."

"Surely that is dangerous?" put in someone.

"Why? They are infidels, but they are also renegades, and, like us, they wish, more than anything else, to see the downfall of our enemies. They have received sanctuary here, and will serve us well. But no more now. That is all I am permitted to tell, except that it is I who have been honoured by being commanded by the Great One to drive the car which will take him to Alexandria to-morrow morning, and at our next meeting I shall have more to tell you.

"Big things are coming, comrades! See to it that each of us is ready to do his part as called upon. And should any wish to draw out, let him remember the oath of the society, and the penalty which will be meted out to all traitors. We live for the glory of Allah and Egypt! Lucky is he who dies in the Cause!"

And at that there was a deep murmur of fanatical praise of Allah, accompanied by a fervent cursing of the British.

Then, from scraping sounds which reached him along the wire, the old beggar knew that the conspirators were about to make a move. He sat up as if he had just woke, and, stretching himself, got to his feet. He picked up his bundle of rags and started at a shambling walk in the direction of the temple.

He was about half-way there when the group of ten appeared. They came towards him at a brisk pace, and long before they reached him he had begun to call down the blessings of Allah upon them, and to plead for alms.

They paid no attention to him until he ran along beside them, pestering them to anger with his cries and moans.

Then one of them cursed him, and struck out at him; another and another followed suit, and then, from under one white burnous, a coin was thrown to him.

The old beggar took the cuffs without a whimper, calling further blessings upon them as he scrambled in the sand for the coin.

When they were past he shuffled along on his way in the direction of the pyramid where he had been lying down.

His coin was only a copper piece, and his effort could not have been called exactly profitable from a financial point of view, but while he had been pestering them he had been close enough to catch a glimpse of the features of each one, and any time in the future he would be able to pick any of the ten out of a crowd and say: "This is he! This is one of the group which was in the small funerary temple by the Pyramids on a certain night—"

When they had quite disappeared in the direction of the Meni House Gate, the desert rat again squatted by the spot where he had been lying down.

He scraped away the sand from the black box he had buried, and replaced it in the basket after disconnecting the end of the wire. This he took in his hands, and in the same, slow way, on his haunches, he began making his way back to the temple, gathering up the wire and recoiling it as he went.

At last he reached the spot where he had buried the microphone and crimped receiver, and, after pulling these out of the shallow hole, he placed them carefully in the basket.

That done, he rose to his feet and started along in the direction of the Meni House.

He was within twenty yards of that spot, when suddenly a big black car came along from the direction of Cairo.

A gentleman in evening dress descended, and assisted a woman, also in evening dress, to alight. Then they set off walking at a leisurely pace towards the Great Pyramid, and after them shuffled the old beggar.

They paid no attention to him, and he did not get close enough to stir the man into physical action.

But he was close enough to them to note when they met a horseman who suddenly appeared from the desert, and to see the hooked nose and forked beard beneath the person's burnous as the moonlight fell on his features.

CHAPTER 6.

The Black Eagle was quite correct in informing Madame Goupolis that the young man in the restaurant at Shepheard's that evening was the same youth she had seen at Monte Carlo some weeks before.

It says something for the sharp eyes of the woman that she noticed the similarity, for she had had only two brief glimpses of him then, and on one occasion it had been only by the reflection of a villa light at night.

And outwardly he was greatly changed.

Not only did he carry his left arm in a sling— it was understood at the hotel that he met with a serious motoring accident some time before, during which a good many bones had been broken—but he looked very drawn and haggard, and his face was chalky white.

Moreover, he was troubled by a hard, dry cough, which caused those who heard it to look at him in a sympathetic manner, for that cough seemed to be nothing less than the protest of lungs considerably advanced in tubercular trouble.

It was a shocking change in one who had been so robust such a short time before, but as it was somehow understood that one of his ribs had penetrated the lung at the time of the accident, his rapid decline was explained.

He had arrived at Shepheard's only a few days before, accompanied by a servant who bore the stamp of being an old batman, and, when he was not in the company of the crowd of young people with whom he had struck up a friendship, this solicitous attendant was to be seen hovering about him.

Which, of course, gave rise to the gossip that his master, the famous Grant Rushton, had sent him to Egypt in the care of a trusted man, in the hope that the dry air of the country would do him good— he himself being too pressed with urgent business affairs to leave England just then.

It was Tony right enough, and certainly he looked ghastly ill. He showed signs of forced gaiety when in the company of other younger folks, and they, on their part, seemed to have formed a conspiracy to keep him cheerful and amused.

But when he was alone his expression was sad enough, and it might have been noticed that at times a sudden feverish impatience would seize him, which caused him to spring up and seek the privacy of his own room without the slightest warning.

On the night in question, however, he seemed more cheerful than usual, though his cough was as bad as ever.

He had dined with the other young people, as Madame Goupolis and the Black Eagle had seen him, and afterwards he had loitered about the lounge instead of going in to watch the dancing.

He, of course, dared not risk indulging in that pleasure for fear of getting overheated, and thus making his position worse.

Another young fellow and his sister had elected to sit in the lounge with him, and the three of them were engaged in a not very exciting game of cards when the Black Eagle and Madame Goupolis passed through.

The Black Eagle had slipped on a silk-lined overcoat and soft crush hat, while the Greek woman had drawn a velvet evening cloak about her shoulders.

These were all the signs that they intended going out, and since the drive out to the Meni House and back was one of "the things" to do after dinner, it was not difficult to guess that they might be bound in that direction.

Scarcely had they disappeared through the door leading to the wide glassed-in veranda, when Tony's servant appeared. He marched up to the young detective, and, standing at attention, respectfully suggested that he had had rather a long day, and should retire early.

Tony merely grunted in reply, and then, as if suddenly seized by one of his feverish impulses, he sprang to his feet.

"I've got it!" he exclaimed, and then broke off as a fit of coughing seized him. The others waited sympathetically until the spasm was over, and then Tony went on:

"It's too early to turn in yet, Mossop. Get my coat and a cap, and I'll go for a run first. What do you say, Jack? And you, Molly? Shall we take a drive out to the Meni House Gate and back? It is a lovely moonlight night."

"If you are sure you won't take cold," said the girl doubtfully, as she looked first at Tony and then at her brother.

"Just as Molly says," was Jack's comment, and Tony laughed.

"I won't take cold," he said cheerfully. "I'm really all right. Mossop here coddles me too much. You buzz off, Mossop, and get my coat and cap, and while you and Molly get your things, Jack, I'll order a car in the office." And before they could argue the point he was speeding towards the reception office.

By the time he had arranged for a car from the rank and inspected it at the door, his man Mossop was back with a heavy coat and cap. He assisted Tony into it, and as he solicitously buttoned it about him his eyes held those of Rushton's assistant for one brief moment.

Just then, as Tony bent forward to let the man get at the collar, he breathed half a dozen words which did not carry past Mossop's ears, and the faintest of nods was the only sign that Mossop had noticed.

Then Jack Torrance and his sister Molly arrived, and the three passed out to the front where the car was waiting.

They piled into the back, and the next moment the car was off, taking the Meni House road.

There had been no need to tell the driver to pick up speed, for all three knew, that, like every native driver from Suez to Yokohama, he would push the car along at breakneck speed despite what they said.

There were other cars on the road, each with its load of laughing passengers out to take the air under the lovely golden disc of the moon, and once in this line their progress was governed by the cars ahead.

Evidently the key man there had the same idea, for the journey out was more of a wild race than anything else, and by the time they reached the Meni House Gate all three of the young people were ready to get down for a breather.

A good many others had chosen to do likewise, so they were only one of the crowd as they strolled across the moon-washed desert in the direction of the Great Pyramid.

It was at Tony's suggestion that they took a course off at a tangent in order to get away from the others, and avoid the mob of beggars which were howling and moaning all about the place.

They were not the only ones who had had the same brainwave, for as they were along they saw the same lady and gentleman just ahead of them whom they had seen pass through the lounge while they had been playing cards.

They followed them at some little distance, and then suddenly from out of the desert there came a flying horseman.

He drew up his steed at a spot where there were no tourists walking about, and while Tony knew too much about desert life as it actually is to swallow any of the silly "sheik" stuff that some women writers hand out to their readers, he had to confess that that white-

34

clad, motionless figure, sitting his horse in the moonlight like a statue, was certainly a romantic and impressive-looking figure.

Molly Torrance thought so, too, for she gave a little cry of pleasure, and said:

"Look, Jack. Look Tony. There is a real, live sheik. Let us walk that way and get a close-up of him."

Tony grinned at Jack.

"Come on then," he said, "if Molly wants some of the sheik stuff, let her have it."

So they started off in that direction, and as they did so they saw that the man and woman ahead of them had apparently been struck with the same idea, for they, too, were making for the spot where the burnoused figure was sitting his horse.

Tony and his two companions were still some distance away when the pair reached the bedouin and seemed to engage him in conversation.

There was another figure near the spot, and as the three young people approached he came shuffling towards them.

Molly gave a little murmur of disgust as the filthy desert rat began to pester them for alms, and Jack took her arm to hurry her on.

But Tony thrust his hand in his pocket, and, taking out a coin tossed it to the beggar.

The latter began to call down blessings of Allah upon him while Jack and his sister were still moving away, and then suddenly the old beggar broke off, and shot out half a dozen swift words in a whisper which caused Tony to give a start and bend forward as if he would say something.

But as he did so the other emitted a sharp hiss, and again his voice rose as he called down the blessings of Allah upon his benefactor.

With that Tony walked on to join his companions who had now stopped to wait for him, and it was just then he saw that the "sheik" had evidently had enough of his survey of tourists, for he had whirled about and was dashing off into the desert at a rapid gallop.

The man and woman who had held him in conversation had turned, and were walking back towards the Meni House Gate, so with some remark about it being too bad that Molly had missed a "close-up" of the sheik, Tony swung in the opposite direction and got them moving off at a tangent in the direction of the Great Pyramid.

They idled about the lower "courses" for a little time, but at last the hordes of beggars became such a nuisance that they retired in disgust. They walked back to the Meni House Gate, where they had left the car waiting, and, getting in, started back towards Cairo.

When they re-entered the lounge Jack and his sister wanted Tony to sit with them for a bit, but the lad excused himself, saying that he thought he had better go to his room, and, as Mossop was to be seen hovering in the background as if keeping an eye out for his charge, they did not press him.

So Tony bade them good-night, and made for the lift. On his way he caught sight of the Black Eagle and Madame Goupolis sitting in one corner of the lounge looking through at the dancers, but they did not see him, and he took good care that they had no chance to do so. He signed Mossop, and told the man to come up in the lift with him.

Once he was in his room Tony made an abrupt gesture for Mossop to close the door. Then he spoke, using a very low tone:

"Have a look in the bath-room and out on the gallery at the back, Mossop. Then come back —I want to talk to you."

The man made a thorough search of the adjoining bath-room and the gallery which ran at the back of Tony's room, overlooking the garden. Then he returned to announce that all was clear. Tony motioned for him to draw close, then:

"I have just seen the guv'nor," he said in a whisper. "Never got a bigger shock in my life —he was hanging about at the Pyramids, got up as an old desert rat, and I wouldn't have spotted him in a thousand years if he hadn't given me the high sign. But I have been expecting to hear from him for the past two days. All he said was for me to carry out my end of the game, and wait until he made some sign. He couldn't have known I would be out at Meni House Gate to-night; but I suppose if he hadn't seen me there he would have got word to me here somehow. But the main thing is, Mossop, that I must get busy to-night." The man, one of the most trusted Secret Service men under the British Government, nodded his head slowly.

"I've been looking for something to break, too," he said. "What is the next move? Did Mr. Rushton say?"

"There wasn't much chance for him to say anything but reveal his identity and make a rendezvous for later. He named that old hut known as the 'Thieves' House,' about half-way out on the Meni House Road. I shall go there."

"In disguise, I take it?"

"Sure. I'll get into that Arab's outfit and get away by the garden. I can't say when I'll be back, or what the next move will be; but you had better stick on duty here, Mossop, until I get back."

The man turned obediently, but as he went he murmured wistfully:

"I'll stay, of course, but just the same I wish I could go with you. It isn't exactly exciting acting as nurse to a young man who is supposed to be in the last stages of consumption and who is really as husky as a stallion."

Tony laughed.

"You'll get action soon enough in this game," he said, "or I miss my guess. And don't you think it has been any fun for me going around trying to scare up a graveyard cough, and shoving this darned white muck on my face every day. Now get busy, Mossop, and I'll strip."

The man entered the small adjoining "servant's room" which Tony had engaged for him, and Tony got out of his dinner clothes.

He turned on the hot water and scrubbed off the white pomade which he had been putting on each day to add colour to the impression that he was ill.

He had just finished when Mossop returned with some white cotton garments on one arm, and in a few minutes Tony had clad himself as any one of the thousands of Arabs or Egyptians who were to be seen anywhere in Cairo.

When he had finished he strapped a holster under his left arm, and examined the clip of his automatic to see that it was full.

Then he turned to Mossop.

"All ready for the stain," he announced.

The man, an expert in such matters, took up a small bottle which contained a dark brown stain, and in the space of a few minutes he had effectually covered all the visible portion of Tony's skin with the stuff.

When he had finished the change was startling, for Rushton's assistant looked exactly what he professed to be, and it would have taken a very keen eye indeed to see through the disguise. Its effectiveness was as much in its simplicity as anything else.

Tony waited again while Mossop explored the veranda at the back, and in a few moments he returned to sign that the coast was clear.

While he was outside he had hung a light but strong silk ladder from the balcony, and Tony wasted no time in getting over the rail.

He went down swiftly, and as he dropped to the turf beneath he gave the ladder a little shake to signal to Mossop to draw it up.

Then he dodged across the garden, taking advantage of every inch on the way, and in less than half a minute he was well away from the lights of the hotel.

He passed the servant's quarters without being seen, and slipped through the gate at the rear of the garden into a lane which ran at the back.

He knew his way perfectly.

Not only had he and Rushton both used that means of egress more than once in the past, but he had examined it carefully since his return to Cairo on this occasion, planning ahead as Rushton had taught him, in anticipation of anything that might arise.

And he knew quite well where the "Thieves' House" was on the Meni House Road. .

Rushton had pointed it out to him several times when they were motoring past, and had told him anecdotes about the notorious hut. They were all of byegone days, for of recent years the place had remained uninhabited.

During the time the Australian troops were quartered in Cairo and Heliopolis, during the War, they had raided the place again and again for the sheer fun of the thing, and had so effectually put the fear of Hades into the vagabonds and rogues who used it, that the place had literally been taboo since then. And it hadn't taken Grant Rushton long to discover that when he was poking about the desert around the Pyramids.

It was, of course, out of the question for Tony to take any sort of wheeled conveyance out to the place. A native of the class he was supposed to be would not have the money for such a thing, so the only thing to do was to hoof it out as rapidly as he could.

It was a trifle over a couple of miles, and although it was not too pleasant walking in the coarse native shoes he had donned, he set out at a brisk pace, and about half an hour after he had struck the Meni House Road he saw the lonely looking grey ruin off in the sand to his left.

It was getting late now, and he had passed scarcely a car on the way out. The after-dinner crowd had returned to their respective hotels, and those who might be dancing out at the Heliopolis Palace or the Meni House would not be coming back for another hour or so.

He had seen a few natives trudging along into Cairo, and had allowed one group to pass him as they came along at a better pace than that at which he was travelling.

But just now the road seemed quite deserted, and after a cautious look in each direction he slid down the gutter at the left and scrambled up the sandbank on the other side. When he was over that he made straight for the grey blur which he knew marked the ruins known as the "Thieves' House."

CHAPTER 7.

There was no sign of life about the place as Tony approached, but he kept on until he was actually in the shadow of one of the walls, and at the sound of his feet slurring the sand, a bat swept out from one of the gaping holes that once might have been a window. That sign meant that Rushton had either not arrived, or, if he had, he was lying very quiet. And Tony chose to think the latter.

He leant in through the hole, and gave a low whistle. Almost at once there came an answering whistle from the darkness inside, and, a second or so later, Tony could see a small patch of light over in one corner as Rushton pressed the switch of an electric torch and held it in an inverted position so the light would beat down close on to the mud floor.

Tony slid over the broken stone sill and walked towards the patch of light. He squatted down close to it, and for a brief moment the man in the shadow swung the circle on to his features.

Then he released the switch, and the only illumination then was what bit of moonlight came through the old window.

"You did well to get here so soon," whispered Rushton. "I figured you might find it difficult to get away from your friends."

"I left them as soon as I got back to the hotel, guv'nor," whispered the young man in reply. "Mossop was on the look-out for me, so I managed to get into this outfit at once. Then I hoofed it out on the road as fast as I could. But, hell's bells, guv'nor, you did give me a shock when you spoke to me at the Pyramids. I knew you would communicate with me, somehow when you were ready, but I didn't look for you in this outfit."

Rushton smiled in the darkness, but his assistant could not see him. Then he went on:

"I have been hanging out there for some days. Almost the first day I got to Cairo I struck a promising trail, and it lead in that direction. I had a little trouble at first trying to keep the pitch I had picked to myself, but after one encounter they left me alone."

Then he related the incident of the horned toads, at which Tony chuckled.

"How has the illness pose gone off?" asked Rushton abruptly.

"Not a hitch, I think, guv'nor. But it's a poor game trying to kick up a consumptive cough every five minutes or so. Mossop has been splendid and I don't think anyone suspects the truth. And I have quite a little to report of what has happened since we parted in London"

"Good, that was why I told you to come out here to-night. Things are moving and in any event, I should have got word through to you to-night. But it was a bit of luck that you happened to go out to Meni House this evening. Now let me have your report, Tony."

"Well, guv'nor, after you left London, I went to see Sir James Fraser, the lung specialist, as you instructed me. I explained what was needed and he fixed me up all right. The next day all the London papers had something about the accident I had had, and I must say some of them played it up for all it was worth. Then I slid out of town and made for Marseilles.

"I came across to Alexandria and on to Cairo, and when we got to Shepheard's I left it to Mossop to spread about the hotel what was necessary. In the meantime I was practising on the cough, and I think I got away with it all right. I should have said that Mossop joined me at Jermyn Street the night before I left.

"Well, nothing happened up till then; nor is there anything to report until I come to a few days ago. Then an old friend of ours came into the hotel one day for lunch, and from that moment I kept an eye on her."

"Of whom do you speak?"

"That Greek woman—Madame Goupolis."

"Yes, I know she is back in Cairo, but go on."

"I don't think she was staying at Shepheard's that first day, but she moved in the next morning and Mossop spotted her room. She has been there since. Well, I and Mossop haven't lost sight of her for more than a few minutes since then. For a day or so she did nothing of a suspicious nature; but the day before yesterday someone else came to the hotel, and she had a good many conversations with that person. I am referring to Archie Pherison, one of the Three Musketeers."

"Ah, that is distinctly interesting, Tony, what else?"

"Of course, I don't know what passed between them guv'nor, but I am positive that they were discussing something of an important and very private nature, for Pherison was in her sitting-room a good deal. I had to keep out of sight as much as possible, and leave the hotel trailing to Mossop; but he had them under surveillance most of the time. Then Pherison left, and Mossop says he took the train to Alexandria."

"Another interesting item."

"Yesterday another person came to the hotel, and he had not been there more than two hours before he and Madame Goupolis were as thick as thieves."

"Are you referring to the Black Eagle, who was out at the Pyramids with her this evening?"

"Yes, but I didn't know you had spotted him there."

"I did though."

"They have been together almost all the time since he came, and this afternoon Madame Goupolis went out on what I think was an important visit."

"Did you follow her?"

"No. I was shadowing the Black Eagle. But Mossop followed the woman."

"I think I can tell you where she went. She went, I believe, to the house of Prince Menes."

"Great Scott! How did you know that, guv'nor?"

"I have not been idle, Tony," responded Rushton dryly. "If that was what Mossop reported you may skip it."

"That was it. And that is all there is to report, except that she and the Black Eagle dined together to-night, and I am pretty certain she was talking to him about me. At any rate, she seemed to call his attention to me."

"Did the good Mossop tell you that Prince Menes was back in Cairo?"

"No, guv'nor; only that she had gone to a house which he was able to identify as belonging to Menes."

"Well, I can supplement that, for Menes is back. Where he has been since he was deported from England a few weeks ago I do not know. But he is in Cairo now—or was when the Goupolis visited him this afternoon. I don't think we need worry even if the Greek woman did recognise you. If your pose has been accepted, then she will hardly be suspicious at seeing you alone at Shepheard's. And, besides, you are not likely to remain there much longer, for things are marching."

"I'm glad of that. What is the next step, guv'nor?"

"I wish I knew. Things have become more complicated than ever. Each hour seems to bring some new element into this business, and, if I had suspected one-tenth of what I know now I would have asked for at least three more specials from the Secret Service. But we have tackled it, and I suppose we must go on with it."

"When you were walking across from the Meni House Gate to-night did you see the Black Eagle and Madame Goupolis stop and exchange some words with a mounted Bedouin?"

"We could see that they were talking to some horseman."

"I managed to get fairly close at that moment, and in one brief moment, when the moonlight fell on that horseman's features, I had a full view of them. And I recognised him."

"Recognised him, guv'nor!" exclaimed Tony. "Recognised that Bedouin! Who on earth was it?"

"Flash Brady."

"B-Brady!" stammered the young detective, almost speechless in amazement. "But I thought Brady was with Abdel Krim in Morocco, hundreds and hundreds of miles from here."

"So did I—until to-night," answered Rushton grimly. "But it was Brady—Brady, with his darkened skin and forked beard and burnous just as he looks as Sakr-el-Droog, the Hawk of the Peak in the Riff country in Morocco. And I am equally certain that his presence here in Egypt at a time like this, in Cairo, when Madame Goupolis is here, talking with that intriguing white devil just after she has seen Menes, bodes no good for our business.

"Little did I dream that these factors would crop up when I left London. You say that a few days ago Archie Pherison, one of the Three Musketeers, was at Shepheard's, and in close conversation with the Greek woman. Following that the Black Eagle, who was mixed up with that Monte Carlo affair with her, turns up, and they are as thick as thieves together. Then she visits Prince Menes, the worst enemy England and the real Egypt ever had, and no sooner does she return than she and the Black Eagle motor out to Meni House Gate to a rendezvous with Flash Brady. Good heavens. Is every British renegade out of gaol mixed up in this?"

"S'truth, it certainly looks like getting complicated," remarked Tony, who had not yet recovered from the shock of discovering that the mysterious desert horseman was none other than Brady. He knew Rushton would not be so positive unless he was dead certain that he was right.

But what Brady was doing so far from Morocco he could not fathom.

Either he had come from the Riff the whole way along the north

43

coast of Africa by steamer, and had landed on some lonely spot on the Egyptian coast near the Tripoli border, or else he must have come overland the full distance, which would mean that he would have to traverse Morocco from the Riff, then Algiers, Tunisia, and finally Tripoli before reaching Egypt.

Of course, Tony knew that with letters from Abdel Krim, the Lion of the Riff, written before his downfall, he would be able to travel straight through the heart of the desert, would be handed from one tribe to another, and would not have to make a single appearance in either the settled part of French Algeria, French Tunisia, or Italian Tripoli.

He had dropped into silence then, pondering on this puzzle and waiting for Rushton to go on, when he was brought back to things with a jerk as Rushton shot out his hand and gripped him by the arm.

Something told Tony to turn, and as he did so he saw the bulky silhouette of a burnoused figure almost filling the broken, irregular oblong of the window.

And even as he gazed the figure bent and began to come over the sill.

CHAPTER 8.

Tony's instinct was to get at his automatic, but something in the pressure of Rushton's fingers made him remain still.

He sensed that Rushton was making no move to challenge the intruder, and he was puzzled.

Yet, he reflected, the Old Thieves' house was Rushton's present stamping ground, so to speak, and he figured that his master ought to know what he was about.

But Rushton was not quite as motionless as the young detective thought, for suddenly the electric torch flashed, and the rays fell full upon the upper portion of the body of the man who was now over the sill, and Tony could see, standing just inside the window.

For a second only the light remained on him, and then the place was plunged into darkness again.

Immediately after Tony heard Rushton's whisper cutting the silence.

"Straight across here in the corner," was what he said, and at that there was a shuffling sound as the man by the window came across the room.

As he moved the oblong of the window was once more revealed, and the next thing Tony was aware of was that someone was getting down on the mud floor beside him.

Then again Rushton spoke in a whisper.

"My assistant Tony is here. You will feel him beside you. Did you have any difficulty?"

"None whatever," came an answering whisper. "I got your message earlier in the evening, and timed myself to get here at the time you mentioned. I had one slight adventure just as I was leaving the road one of the gang was spying about and tried to follow me—it came to grips, and I was forced to wring his neck." Tony twisted his head in the dark as he heard the newcomer speak in such casual fashion of wringing the neck of one of the native murder gang, but, of course, he could see nothing but a faint blur where the other sat.

He had no idea of the identity of the stranger, but he had heard enough by now to know that he must be an Englishman, and, he shrewdly suspected, a Secret Service agent with whom Rushton had made an appointment.

As a matter of fact, the lad's deductions were correct, for the man beside him was none other than Lawrence Malone, famous explorer and at times most trusted secret agent of the British Government. It was unusual for Malone to be on a job in that part of the world, however.

He was employed mostly on the China coast when there was some particularly delicate mission to handle.

And not even Rushton knew exactly how and why Malone had got into Egypt on the same job as himself.

He had been told in London when he had been asked to go out to Egypt on this mission, which was one of the most dangerous he had ever tackled, that he might find Malone there.

He had been given a code figure and address by which he might get into touch with Malone if he desired to do so, and on reaching Cairo he had lost no time in doing so. His business was to ferret out one phase of the murderous conspiracy which was widespread in the country; Malone's was to handle another phase of it.

And this was the third occasion on which the pair had compared notes in that dilapidated old "Thieves' House" on the Meni House Road. But, of course, Tony knew nothing of that.

Rushton murmured something at what Malone said, and then he went on:

"I have struck something definite at last. I thought you would be the best person to handle it. I suspected what was afoot last night, and that is why I sent a message to you this afternoon. It was just a chance whether I should get hold of anything to-night or not. But I did, and it is important."

"Good man!" whispered Malone. "What have you struck?"

"I will tell you." Rushton paused, and then, in an aside, said: "This is Mr. Lawrence Malone, Tony. He is on the same job." Then he added to Malone: "My assistant is handling his end of the job at Shepheard's, and has made a most valuable report this evening. I shall tell you about that later. But to get back to what I discovered."

"I knew that some of the murder gang had been meeting recently outside Cairo. I couldn't discover where it was for some days; but at last I spotted something that looked suspicious, and last night I tracked them down. They have been meeting in one of those funerary temples between the Great Pyramid and the other two, which have been brought to light only recently by the American expedition which is working there.

"I managed to make a pretty thorough survey of the place during the day, and to-night I rigged up a microphone near the entrance. I attached this to a crimped receiver, and brought a wire from that for about a hundred and fifty yards under the sand to a spot near the lowest course of one of the smaller pyramids where I have been hanging out as a beggar.

"I was lucky. There was a full meeting tonight of one of the sections. It is by no means one of the inner gang; but there is mischief afoot to-morrow, and this lot has been chosen to do the job. Do you know Lushington of the Lands Department?"

"Yes," whispered Malone.

"It is Lushington, they have planned to murder him to-morrow. There is a bad leakage from Lushington's office, though I can't tell you the name of the culprit. But I can tell you exactly what is planned for to-morrow, and the names of the four who have been chosen to do the killing."

"That is a big thing, Rushton," said Malone. "The first trick goes to you. It is what I have been looking for and been unable to find. You say you can give me the actual names?"

Rushton handed him a piece of paper.

"Yes," he said, "I have jotted them down on this piece of paper. Here it is. I shall tell you them now, as well, but I daresay they will mean nothing to you."

Then Rushton gave the four names he had heard spoken as the drawing took place in the temple.

When he had finished Malone acknowledged that he could not recollect having heard them before, and Rushton went on:

"The murder is planned for between a quarter-past one and half-past one in the afternoon. They know to a minute every move which Lushington is to make to-morrow. It seems that he has an appointment at the Residency at half-past one, and will leave the Lands Office at about ten minutes or a quarter-past one. His car will go by certain streets, and at about a quarter or twenty minutes past one it will pass the corner of the street, the name of which I have written down on that piece of paper. It is there that the four assassins will be in wait for it, and it is there that they plan to do the murder.

"Just round the corner another car will be waiting, and it is by this they expect to escape. That car, if it gets away, will run them straight out into the desert to a small oasis, which I have also written down, and there they plan to disguise themselves as bedouins. Then they will be rushed across towards the Tripoli border and thus out of the country."

"That may be what they plan, but it isn't what will happen," remarked Malone, grimly. "Thanks to you, Rushton, this is one murder which will not come off as per schedule, and I shall be there personally to see that we bag all four of these dogs of assassins. I'll talk this over with Lushington and see what he has to say. It might be the best plan to have him start off as he has planned, and then to jump the lot of them just before they open up."

"That is what I would suggest, too—if there is no hitch. If they are allowed to begin shooting they might get Lushington before they can be stopped."

"I'll see that they don't. I'll have a score of men in disguise ready to jump them the minute they move. We ought to bag the lot. Can you arrange to be there?"

"No. I am leaving Cairo in the morning. In fact I shall get away as soon now as I can. And in that you can do something for me as soon as you get back to Cairo."

"Of course I shall. What is it?"

"I want a police car, a closed one with good curtains. I want it to come out here as soon as possible and pick me up and Tony, for it is urgent that I get through to Alexandria as quickly as possible."

"Is this on a new trail?"

"It is an old trail that has just been reopened. It means that that dog Menes is back in Cairo, and is already at work."

"The devil he is. I hadn't heard that. How did you find out?"

"In the same way as I discovered what is planned for to-morrow—that and something Tony told me. Menes is going to Alexandria to-morrow, so he won't be here when they try to get Lushington. But I have a hunch that he has other business in Alexandria besides just wanting to be away from Cairo for the day, and I am going to try and find out what it is. There have been several queer things going on which Tony has reported, and I want to investigate them. Also I saw a man tonight who, I suspect, may also be mixed up in this game out here. I can't say anything yet, but as soon as I can get hold of anything definite I shall, of course, let you know. Have you anything new?"

"Yes. I have been keeping it until you finished what you had to say. I don't know that there is anything in it and I haven't been able to get hold of much yet to go on. But a very peculiar thing has occurred. And you will be particularly interested, for the person it concerns is one you know only too well."

"What do you mean, Malone?"

"I mean that Prince Wu Ling is in Cairo."

"Wu Ling in Cairo! Is that possible?"

"It is not only possible, but a fact. He is not travelling in his usual style. On the contrary. He is as retiring as a little spring primrose. But he is here, nevertheless, and I expect to discover before many hours have passed where he is in hiding. I don't know what he can be doing in Cairo. I haven't got far enough yet to try and figure out. But the more I see of this business that is going on here, the more inclined am I to think that he is here to see Menes. It may be on some matter entirely unconnected with our job, but—well, you know even better than I do what Wu Ling is."

Rushton was silent for some little time. What Malone had just told him was, to his mind, of even greater importance than his friend thought. If Wu Ling was in Cairo, and was trying to remain incog., then Rushton knew perfectly well that the Chinaman was not in the place for his health.

So far he had no record of Wu Ling and Menes having joined forces in any of their schemes; but that was no criterion.

From what he had discovered since arriving in Cairo this time, from what he had heard from Malone and from what Tony had reported, it was growing more and more plain to Rushton that there was either a conspiracy about to be born, or in full being, that was on a far more ambitious and gigantic scale than anything he had yet come up against.

Menes, Madame Goupolis and the Black Eagle, Archie Pherison, one of the Three Musketeers. Where there was one of that murderous trio there would the other two be. And Brady! He had seen the latter with his own eyes only that evening, and he had been in conversation with Madame Goupolis and the Black Eagle.

Was it possible that all those renegades and criminals were being drawn into some wide net which Menes was casting? If so, then why not Wu Ling as well?

Wu Ling was a man of a power more widespread even than that which Menes wielded. But that need not prevent him joining forces with the Egyptian if it suited his purpose.

His price would be a high one—money would not gain his service. But there were other things besides money, and if the wily Celestial entered into any bargain he would take care that he got his payment in full.

It was a startling possibility, and just then Rushton wanted to ponder over it alone. He wanted to bring to bear every atom of mental concentration of the thing and try to get hold of some loose end which might lead him somewhere.

And that is why he did not pursue the subject when Malone rose to go.

Before he disappeared through the window he promised to send a secret service car out on the road as soon as he got back to Cairo, and Rushton assured him that he and Tony would be ready.

Then the big explorer was gone, and silence reigned once more, while Rushton sank into deep thought.

But some inner sense seemed to tell him when they should make a move, for it was about an hour and a half later that he roused himself and touched Tony's arm.

They went out through the window like two ghosts, and started off across the sand towards the road.

They had almost reached it when they came upon what looked like a bundle of white rags. But on bending over they saw that it was the huddled figure of a native.

They did not need to extend their examination to know that he was dead. Rushton drew the cotton cloth away from his face and bent closer. Then he rose.

"It is one of the ten who came out of the temple," he said. "Malone did good work when he finished this one off. It is only one less, but every unit counts in the fight we are making against this murder gang. Still, I can't quite figure why he was hanging about here unless he had grown suspicious of me and was spying on me."

"Perhaps he was suspicious of Mr. Malone, and followed him out from Cairo," suggested Tony.

Rushton agreed, and as a matter of fact, it was Tony who was right.

They left him just where he was, for they knew that before the day was very old he would be found and carried off and that nothing more would ever be heard of the incident.

Then they continued on their way, and they had scarcely reached the road, where the trees stretched in two parallel lines the whole way from Cairo to the Meni House Gate, when they heard the low purr of an engine.

A few minutes later a big, black closed car came along and drew up beside them.

The driver said not a word, nor did Rushton.

He saw that the inner curtains had been drawn down, and he knew that the driver was one of the trusted servants in the Secret Service. He also knew that he would have received his instructions from Malone, so he opened the door and motioned Tony to get in.

He followed, and as soon as the door was closed the driver began to turn.

A single electric bulb was burning inside, and by this illumination they could see that Malone had been thoughtful enough to put in a well-packed hamper of food and drink—a godsend, needless to say, to Rushton, who had been living on nothing but kous-kous and dates for days.

Then as the car got round and started back towards Cairo to pick up the Alexandria road, Rushton switched off the light, and they sat in darkness, for none knew better than they the full extent of the peril which attended their every movement at the present time.

CHAPTER 9.

Rushton and Tony kept close behind the seclusion of the drawn blinds the whole way to Alexandria. They did not attack the contents of the hamper until they were many miles out of Cairo and dawn was come.

Then they made an enjoyable meal out of the lavish supplies which Malone had packed, and following that Rushton wrapped up what was left into two paper parcels, one for each to carry under his cloak, for they knew not when they might be able to tackle civilised food again.

Then Rushton discussed with his assistant every phase of the business up to the visit of Malone the night before.

Before leaving Cairo they had stopped just long enough to pass a brief and cryptic message on to a Secret Service patrol, which that agent would convey to Mossop at Shepheard's. It was necessarily vague, for Rushton hadn't the faintest idea when they might return from Alexandria—if they returned at all.

On this job it was a matter of going on the jump whither the trail might lead, and they could not tell from hour to hour what would crop up next.

Rushton would have given a good deal to have learned more about Wu Ling's visit to Cairo. He would have been better pleased, too, had he been able to follow up the path Flash Brady had taken when he had galloped off across the desert in the moonlight.

But in view of what he had heard in the temple he figured his best plan would be to keep as much in the vicinity of Menes as he could.

And if he had heard the truth coming over the wire as he lay on the sand, then Menes intended going to Alexandria that day.

He might have got away before them, or he might be behind them. It was impossible to say. Exactly what would be the next move of the Goupolis and the Black Eagle was a problem, but it all worked round to Menes as the head and tail of the business, and, besides, there was another suggestive line in the fact that Archie Pherison had returned to Alexandria after his several interviews with the Greek woman.

Rushton had a hunch that, by sticking to Menes, he would be nearest the answer of the riddle he was trying to solve, and, further, that the same road would bring him to those others if, as he was beginning to suspect, they were being drawn into the activities of the

White Flag Gang.

If they were not, then he had no interest in them for the present.

His job was to get to the bottom of the murder business with which Egypt was reeking; to put his hands on those higher up—much higher up—who were debauching the minds of silly, fanatical students and turning the country into a murder trap for the British; to snap the invisible cord of crime and treason that was being spun into a web in the Sudan.

And something told him that if he could only get Menes where he wanted him, he would find all that he was seeking.

In passing, it may be stated here that the information which Rushton was able to pass on to Lawrence Malone was proved correct in every detail. While he and Tony were still on the road to Alexandria, Lushington of the Lands Department was going ahead with his appointments for the day, just as he had planned.

This was after he had had a long interview with Malone and others of the Secret Service, and the Lands Department men had insisted on going ahead, as per schedule, despite the fact that he would be taking his life in his hands.

His car left the Lands Department building a little past one o'clock, and it was just on the quarter when it swung down the sandy street towards the corner at the part of the bazaar which had been chosen as the best spot to bring off the assassination.

There was a trusted man at the wheel and he did not falter. He drove on at a moderate pace, and then, just as he swung the corner, four white-clad students sprang out into the road.

From beneath the loose folds of their garments they dragged out automatic pistols and sprang to deliver the fusillade which they had planned should end in just one more "unfortunate murder of a British official in Cairo."

But not a single trigger was pulled.

After them, as close as their own shadows, came the men whom the Secret Service had placed.

Before a single shot was fired they were upon the assassins, and while the car pulled to one side to pass on, police and murderers were rolling in the dust in a deadly struggle.

There could be only one result of that encounter.

Malone had seen that there could be no other.

And while the fanatical, ignorant fools were being subdued, and the handcuffs put on, another small detail of Secret Service men had quietly roped in the driver of the car which had been pulled up round the corner to wait until the deed was done.

It was some days before Rushton heard the story of that and the English papers never heard a whisper of the incident.

It was just one of the many incidents that called for no publicity as long as the crime had been prevented.

But if Rushton had known of it, and had known that the four young natives captured were identified under the same four names which he gave to Malone, he would have had further confirmation of the importance of the rest of the talk which he had overheard the night before.

While Rushton had confessed to Tony that, had he guessed for a single moment that the mission he was on was to develop into an affair of such extent, he would have been better pleased to have had more Secret Service men at his command—he had no cause for complaint as to the arrangements which had been made to entail every secrecy of his movements.

From Alexandria and Port Said to Cairo, and from Cairo up the Nile to Wadi Haifa, and even on from the Sudan to Khartoum, the whole network of the Secret Service police was at his disposal.

He had but to command, and whatever he needed would be forthcoming, and it may be said that, at that time, the whole country was spread over with Secret Service men and spies, for the Government had made up its mind that the atrocious murders which had been taking place must be stopped, once and for all.

And it was just one part of this determination that Grant Rushton had been sent out to handle the most delicate part of the whole business.

Therefore, Rushton knew that he would have no difficulty in going into hiding as soon as they should reach Alexandria.

In fact, he had, in a small oiled wallet about his neck, several thin papers which were his stock-in-trade, and among them was one which contained a plan of Alexandria, and which was covered with a multitude of tiny blue and red and green crosses which told him volumes.

It was after consulting this plan, and fixing one of the crosses in his mind, that Rushton picked up the speaking tube and gave brief instructions to the driver.

The man indicated by a nod of the head that he understood, and thus it was that, as they were approaching Alexandria, he took a side turning to the left, which, according to the plan, should bring them round behind the town and on down towards the harbour.

They passed, soon, through some rather dingy suburbs, and then a small and extremely dirty bazaar.

Following that they struck sandy, open country, and then they came into what was easily the dirtiest collection of hovels in the whole of Alexandria— which is saying a good deal.

It was close in front of one of these that the car drew up, and almost before it had stopped Rushton was out, followed by Tony. They did not pause, but slipped at once through the low doorway of the hut nearest them, and the driver went on immediately.

He had stopped less than half a minute altogether, but even though Rushton knew that, even in that brief space of time, there were many pairs of eyes which had seen them get out and enter the hut, there was little danger that the incident would be reported.

If his information were correct, then the population of that section of the city was composed exclusively of vagabonds and criminals; and while it would undoubtedly excite comment to see two such dirtily clad natives as he and Tony get out of a sumptuous car, such a case would find a dozen different explanations to fit it. And, in any event, it was a risk that had to be taken.

At first it was impossible to see a single thing inside the hut. Outside, the glare of the early afternoon sun was terrific, and even in the few moments that had elapsed from the time they stepped out of the car until they plunged into the hut, they had become momentarily blinded.

But after a few minutes their eyes began to get used to the dim interior, and they could see that the outer room of the place was furnished with nothing more than a rough table and a couple of chairs. There was a low door opposite that by which they had entered, and, with a word to Tony, Rushton crossed and pushed it open.

The place beyond seemed to be in utter darkness, but after fumbling about for a bit Tony discovered a wooden shutter, which he opened.

It let in the daylight, and they could now see that the inner room contained a couple of rough beds, which, in India, would have been called charpoys. They were simply wood frames on legs, with a network of rough cords between the sides and ends of the frame.

There was a small stool in the room, and one chair with a leg missing. That was all—except a very unpleasant odour. Again they caught sight of a small door opposite them, and, on being pushed open, they could see a small yard shut off from those adjoining on either side by a fence of stakes and palm-leaves.

Out in the yard was a small shack, which they knew must be a cookhouse, and after a brief survey of this uninviting scene they returned to the front room.

Rushton motioned for Tony to close the door which gave on to the street, and when the lad had done so Rushton took the risk of lighting a cigarette. As he exhaled the welcome smoke he smiled, the first time Tony had seen his features relax since he had met him near the Meni House Gate.

"Well, old son," he said with a shrug, "we can scarcely call our present quarters luxurious, but I am afraid they will have to serve. Heaven alone knows how long we shall have to make use of them; but, if my information is correct—or, rather, if I have correctly decoded certain signs on the plan which I was studying in the car— we should soon see signs of some person to attend to our wants. In the meantime I shall plot out what we have to do, for there is no time to be lost if we are to pick up Menes' trail.

"Now I am going on the probability that he is really coming to Alexandria to-day. I may be wrong, and this whole journey may be nothing but the wildest of wild goose chases, but we will still play out our hand. The first thing to do is to find out if he has come, or is coming. Did you take note as to how we came after we turned off from the main road?"

"Yes, guv'nor."

"Well, that is your job. I want you to go back to the junction of those roads and keep watch. I am counting on the possibility that Menes would not get away from Cairo as early as we got away. And, even at that, it all depends on whether he uses one of his own cars. The Secret Service possess a record of these, and I shall jot down the numbers of the three before you go."

As he spoke Rushton took out a pencil and a small piece of paper, and then he wrote down the numbers. He gave the slip of paper to Tony and went on.

"Of course he may not risk using one of his own cars. Therefore it will be necessary for you to keep an eye out for every car that passes, coming from the direction of Cairo, and the occupants as well when it is possible for you to catch sight of them. Then if you see anyone or any car that makes you think it might be Menes, come back here at once. Myself, I shall go into the City. I want to sort out things there and have a look along the waterfront. I have an idea in my mind that I want to test. So we shall make a rendezvous to meet again here. If you get back first, wait for me, and if I return first, I shall be here when you come. Have you got all that clear?"

"Perfectly, guv'nor."

"Very well, then— But, wait a moment; I think I hear someone in the back room."

Scarcely had Rushton made a cautioning gesture to Tony, when the door leading to the back room was pushed open, and an old, old native woman entered.

She hobbled across to them, peering uncertainly through the gloom. Then Rushton spoke, using Egyptian Arabic.

"You are looking for something, mother," he said. "Can I assist you?"

The old woman paused abruptly, and tapped her stick on the floor. Then she drew a little closer, and bent forward to peer more closely at the speaker.

"The house is empty and there is no food, but by the grace of Allah, who is all-bountiful, and to whom all be praised, there will soon be food and drink and money for these poor old hands to touch. Is that not so, my son?"

"It is so, mother, if you serve us well. We shall want clear, cold water for the evening, and what simple food you can prepare. We shall also need clean blankets for the beds, for we may occupy the house for some days. Can you see all this is done?"

"Yes, my son, by the will of Allah it shall be done. My grand-daughter, who is young and strong, shall bring clean, cold water, and cook the food. My grandson, who is a lusty young dog, shall be at hand to do what is ordered. And this shall be if there is silver for my old hand to touch, for it is many a long day since these fingers have caressed the metal."

"It shall be, then," responded Rushton. "But no money for your fingers to touch until everything is ready."

The old woman mumbled, and then, without another word,

hobbled away. When she was gone Tony looked at Rushton in a puzzled way.

"Most of it was in code talk," said Rushton in a low voice. "She was quite as old as she looks, but she is loyal to the core, and her whining for money was for the benefit of anyone who might have been listening outside. Her husband and her three sons served with the Colours. She is rich, as natives go, but she hates the White Flag gang and all their murderous plots, and she has chosen voluntarily to come into this filthy and dangerous district as a secret agent. She can be trusted to the limit, and she can show us half a dozen different ways of getting away if we need to go on the run. Now be off, my lad. We have no time to waste."

And, marvelling at it all, even though he had plenty of experience of the same type of thing, Tony went.

CHAPTER 10.

The city of Alexandria is one of the oldest and most important seaports along the whole length of the Mediterranean.

It was one of the first places which the adventurous Phoenicians of old discovered when they set out in their tiny craft to see what the blue waters which stretched away from the coast of Asia Minor might reveal, just as, a little later, when they had extended their journeys far to the west, they eventually packed up all their household goods, and, taking their women and children with them, cruised along the north coast of Africa to found Carthage, which later became so famous under that wonderful general of old, Hannibal.

That was long before Ænius with Ascanius and Anchises made his wonderful odyssey, which Virgil has immortalised, and when he found Carthage grown to a great and important city under Queen Dido.

But even then Alexandria was of considerable importance as a seaport of Egypt, and a little later, as history goes, the Greeks poured into the city of promise, and made it vastly wealthy as a commercial centre.

Following that, the arts sought it out and, before the disastrous fire which took place when it was sacked, and when the great library containing over half a million volumes of irreplaceable works of the ancients was destroyed, it was easily the metropolis of the Eastern Mediterranean.

Its decline came with the rise of the Romans and the march of the conquering Greeks across Asia.

It stagnated for centuries, more or less, but still there was always a cunning commercial element to be found there, and with the more modern prosperity of Egypt under the British, with the building of the Suez Canal, which again opened up direct communication between the Mediterranean and the Indian Ocean by way of the Red Sea (for the first time since one of the Pharaohs had made a canal from the Nile into the Bitter Lakes), prosperity again came to it, and to-day, if it is not in the same rank of importance as Marseilles, it can certainly run Barcelona and some of the Italian ports a close race, while it overtops the ports of Greece, and even Constantinople.

That is what the cotton development by the British has done for Egypt.

Grant Rushton knew the port intimately. Aside from having

stepped off many times on his way into and out of Egypt, he had been there on several occasions on cases, and he made it his business to learn all he could about the city.

Therefore, when he left the hut in the terrible quarter of thieves and vagabonds, which he had chosen as a retreat for the time being, he knew just how to get down to the harbour front in the least possible time.

He was still clad in the filthy beggar's rags which he had worn back in Cairo, for he could not have found a safer disguise just then for the part he was playing.

He was certainly a very disreputable figure as he shuffled his way along through the criminal quarter and on to a somewhat more respectable part of the town.

But in that country of dirt and beggars and vagabonds he created no particular notice at all, except to bring down upon his head a stream of curses now and then, when he was not quite lively enough in getting out of the way of some greasy Levantine trader.

But this did not worry Rushton. On the contrary.

The more of that sort of thing, the better for his disguise, so it was with a feeling that, so far, his secret was safe, that he finally reached the waterfront, where ships from every quarter of the globe were congregated.

In some ways it reminded him a little of Marseilles, without the efficiency of that port, and, with his knowledge of the place, it did not take him long to pick out a spot from which to begin his tour.

Rushton was looking for something in particular.

His search had been inspired by something which Tony had told him. That was what the lad had to say about the visit of Archie Pherison to Cairo.

Now, those who have read any of the records of Rushton's experiences with the three criminals known as the Three Musketeers, will know that invariably those three young men travelled together.

On that last occasion on which Rushton had been up against them he had brought their activities to an abrupt close by capturing two of them—Archie Pherison, the leader, if leader there was, and Reggie Fetherston. The third, Algy Somerton, had managed to get away, but Rushton had breathed a sigh of relief when he handed Pherison and Fetherston over to the French police authorities.

The capture had been made in the Channel, in French territorial waters, and Rushton had no option but to give the two criminals into the custody of our neighbours, but had he known for a single moment that the latest of the many charges against them in France was just over three years old, he would have managed somehow to get them back into British waters before arresting them.

For be it known that, in France, a charge cannot be brought against a man if the space of three years has been allowed to elapse from the time the crime was committed.

That is quite different from our British law, which makes it possible to charge a man at any time after an offence has been committed.

In France this quirk in the law is sometimes guarded against by a fugitive being tried in "his absence," and if he is found guilty, sentence may be passed accordingly.

In this way he may be taken into custody at any time he may come within the jurisdiction of French law, but to us it seems rather farcical to "try" and "convict" a man who may be safe on the other side of the world and who intends to remain there, for as long as he keeps off French territory he is usually safe enough.

That was the clause in the French penal code which the astute lawyer engaged by Pherison and Fetherston raked up.

Needless to say, the lawyer in question was briefed by the multi-millionaire, Mathew Cardolak, who had his own very good reasons for not wanting the Three Musketeers to be languishing in gaol, and who poured out money like water in order to get them out of the clutches of the law.

In their case they had not been "tried" and "convicted" in their absence, with the result that the examining judge had no option but to release them.

And thus it was that they slid out of France after only a few weeks in the Sante Prison in Paris.

Mathew Cardolak's yacht, with Algy Somerton on board, was waiting out in the Atlantic to receive them and take them to a place of safety, and Grant Rushton had heard nothing more of the trio (except that they were free by a fluke) until Tony told him that he had seen Archie Pherison at Shepheard's, and that he had spent a good deal of time with the Greek woman.

Under ordinary circumstances Rushton would not have attached too much importance to that incident, but in view of the other items which now had to be considered, he was inclined to think the numerous conversations which had taken place between the pair had not had their genesis out of any mere philandering on the part of Pherison, or the natural, instinctive drawing together of two crooks—even granting Madame Goupolis was a very beautiful woman, and attracted men like a honey-pot attracts bees.

If Pherison was in the country, then, Rushton figured, the other two members of the trio could not be very far away.

Mathew Cardolak was not actively a part of his thoughts just then, for he had no idea that the multi-millionaire might be cruising in the Mediterranean.

But, nevertheless, he reckoned it as a possibility that the cunning old man might be somewhere in that part of the world, and that the Three Musketeers might be on some new job for him. Otherwise they would be operating "on their own," as the saying goes.

But if it were possible to link up in any way at all Pherison with the Greek woman, then it was always on the cards that those same links would be part of the chain that connected her with the Black Eagle.

Rushton knew that the latter had been mixed up with her in the affair at Monte Carlo, and Tony had seen that they were constantly together at the hotel, while he, himself, had seen them out at the Pyramids.

That brought Flash Brady into the picture, and it was not unreasonable to think that the same chain might reach to him.

On top of that, Lawrence Malone had given him the startling information that Wu Ling was in Cairo, apparently using every effort to remain incognito, and with all his experience behind him it was not surprising that Rushton was beginning to suspect that he was close—very close—to something of a very sinister and enormously widespread nature.

Which brought him back again to Archie Pherison at one end, as it were, and Menes, the Egyptian, at the other. Could he make each end of the chain connect those two together?

That was exactly what he had been asking himself, and that was what had brought him to Alexandria. For Menes was supposed to be coming to Alexandria that same day.

Rushton made his tour of the waterfront slowly and deliberately. In keeping with his disguise, he was forced to play the part of a beggar from time to time, and, while this brought him more kicks than ha'pence, it served to cover up his real purpose.

Once again he would have welcomed the assistance of an extra Secret Service man, for he knew that Tony should have someone to help him keep watch on the traffic coming from the direction of Cairo, and he himself needed to be about the docks.

But he had to trust that luck would be with his assistant, for even if Menes did come it would be only by the merest fluke that he himself might spot him in the maze of traffic and bustling life on the waterfront.

He had covered about half the curve of the half-moon of the harbour when, all of a sudden, he came to an abrupt halt, and, for the barest fraction of a second, almost straightened up in his own natural stance as he saw a slim, rakish-looking yacht out in the harbour.

He needed no glasses to read the name of that yacht.

He had seen her under too many stirring conditions to be mistaken, and what he saw was sufficient to tell him that in one thing at least his deductions had been sound—in thinking that Mathew Cardolak might be in that part of the world.

For the yacht at anchor was none other than the "Sultan," which belonged to the millionaire.

Rushton made his way along until he got as near to her anchorage as he could, then he chose a spot behind some bales of cotton on one of the wharves, and squatted down where he would not be disturbed.

Seated thus, he began to watch, and though the yacht was a good quarter-mile off shore, he could make out plenty of signs of movement about her decks.

He could also see a small motor-boat bobbing alongside, and he wondered if perhaps Pherison or one of his fellow criminals might be coming ashore.

For the better part of an hour nothing of any interest occurred.

The day was now fading, and the sun was dropping low in the west. Out at the opening of the harbour there was a greyish tinge over the water, which, in that part of the world, meant only one thing.

It meant that the drop of the sun and the coming of the night would bring a heavy, low-hanging mist on the harbour, and Rushton anathematised it accordingly, for once it shut down the yacht would become invisible. Little did he dream then just what the mist was to mean to him before the night was over.

He was still watching sky and water critically when he saw a white-clad figure descend a ladder that hung down the side of the yacht. This individual stepped into the motor-boat, and Rushton could see him signalling his arms to the deck above.

Almost at once a couple of men came tumbling down the ladder, and after a few moments the motor-boat shot away from the side, heading, after a wide, sweeping turn, for the shore.

Rushton stirred a little, getting ready to make his way along, and try to get near, if possible, to the jetty at which she would land. But she seemed to be coming straight in his direction, and a little later he came to the conclusion that she was making for the steps of a landing jetty which was little more than a biscuit-throw from where he sat.

He got up and shuffled along to the head of the wharf. He passed round the bales of cotton, and continued on towards the jetty at which he thought the motor-boat would touch.

And then, just before he reached it, he paused and, assuming a very feeble progress, half stumbled, half fell into a squatting posture on that side of the wharf.

And not all of it needed to be assumed, for something he had seen had been enough to bring him up in sheer amazement.

Across on the other jetty was a small group of persons. They had evidently reached the place without him seeing them, and had signalled out to the yacht to send a boat ashore—which meant that they were going aboard.

If Rushton had needed further confirmation that his mind was functioning in his usual logical way, he got it then, for in the forefront of the group was a tall, thin Egyptian, clad in European clothes all except a crimson tarbush.

There was no attempt at disguise, and Rushton had not the slightest difficulty in recognising the native as none other than Menes himself.

Point one, he thought. And it was, for it was a definite linking up of Menes with the Three Musketeers and Mathew Cardolak.

But that was by no means all. Close behind Menes was another tall figure—his features those of the East, too, but of a very different cast from the Egyptian's. It was Wu Ling, the cunningest and most subtle Chinaman who had ever come out of the Land of the Yellow Dragon, and at sight of his old enemy Rushton knew that Lawrence Malone had made no mistake when he said that the Celestial was in

Cairo.

He and Menes may or may not have motored through from Cairo together; but the fact remained that they were on the jetty together, and that was good enough for Rushton.

Which was point two, he told himself.

Nor was that the end of it. There were two other persons in the little group. One of the two was a woman, and Rushton could see, despite the fact that she was half-turned from his line of vision, that it was Madame Goupolis. The other was the Black Eagle!

Which made points three and four!

Quite an interesting little gathering, so Rushton thought; nor did he find his interest one whit abated when, a few minutes later the motor-boat from the "Sultan" touched the steps of the jetty, and Archie Pherison came hurrying along to the group.

Rushton watched with a drooping eye while Pherison greeted them and ushered them down into the boat. Then Rushton saw several natives in the garb of servants standing by some bits of luggage, and, after some conversation with Menes, Archie Pherison ran back up the steps and said something to the men.

Rushton gathered that he was telling them he would send the boat back for the luggage, and, as a matter of fact, he was right.

Then Pherison re-entered the boat, which immediately started and headed out towards the yacht.

As Rushton watched it go bobbing along he saw the threat of the night mist was even more pronounced than ever. He was in a quandary just what to do.

He knew that Tony would probably be back at the hut by now, and, no matter what move he decided on, he must go back to his assistant as he had promised, for he would need him that evening.

This contretemps which had arisen upset all his calculations. He could not have dared to hope to come upon as much as he had seen in those few minutes, and he was naturally elated that his instinct and reasoning had led him so truly.

Nevertheless, he was not exactly prepared to tackle such complications on the spur of the moment.

He had figured on finding out whether Menes had arrived in Alexandria, and then having time to plan out what he would do. But he had certainly not figured out on seeing four of the suspected on the jetty at the same time, and he had been forced to stand by and watch them pass under his very nose without being able to do a thing towards following them.

For a few minutes he pondered upon the possibility of going out with the servants and the luggage. But he soon dismissed this as out of the question. Menes was not the sort to have such slack servants as that in his employ.

But he knew, as surely as the sun had just disappeared beneath the rim of the sea, that there would be things said there out on board the yacht during the coming evening that would be of untold value to him and to the British Government.

And if it cost him his life he was determined to make a supreme effort to find out what was going on.

He fumed and fretted as he squatted on his haunches, trying, along every channel which his fertile mind could suggest, to hit on some plan which might at least have one chance in a thousand of success.

He was still there when dusk deepened to darkness, and the threatening mist came in a low, white, sullen bank, over the face of the harbour, blotting out every anchored craft from his view.

Then an idea came to him, and he rose.

He shuffled along past the jetty where Menes' servants were still waiting, and kept on to a long wharf where the harbour boatmen were accustomed to congregate, and from which point of vantage they dash out in their shrieking hordes to swarm about every fresh arrival in the harbour.

The mist was not so thick inshore, but by the time he was forty or fifty yards away from the jetty he had just left, it was invisible, and that is why he did not see another figure step upon it and stand looking out seawards.

Had he done so he would have known that still a fifth guest to be taken to the yacht had turned up, and that, although the newcomer was dressed in white lower garments and a voluminous white burnous which he had drawn about his head and face, it was the same man he had seen in the saddle by the Great Pyramid the preceding evening.

That person had been Flash Brady, or, as Rushton knew him more recently, Sakr-el-Droog, which means Hawk of the Peak.

Which would have made point number five had he but known.

CHAPTER 11.

When Rushton climbed the rising streets which led up from the harbour the moon had already risen, and, standing at one point, he could look down over the lights of the town on to the great white blanket of mist which seemed to lie like one great tablecloth over the harbour.

It did not rise into the main town, but seemed to hold back at the water's edge; nevertheless, it was dense enough to conceal all the shipping at anchorage.

It might lift as suddenly as it had come in from the sea, but that, Rushton knew, would depend on whether a land breeze sprang up or not. He studied it for a while, then he continued on his way.

On reaching the hut which he and Tony were making their temporary headquarters, he found the young man seated in one of the chairs in the front room, his only illumination being what moonlight filtered in through the half-open door. He had been on watch for Rushton, and shot out an eager whisper as his employer shuffled in.

Rushton waited until he was close to where his assistant was sitting before he made reply. Then:

"Has the old woman been in?" he asked, countering the question for the moment.

"Yes, guv'nor, she came in and took a look at me. She didn't say anything, nor did I. I fancy she was waiting for you to return. I've something to report."

"What is it?"

"I spotted Menes' car all right, guv'nor. At least, a car bearing one of the numbers you gave me went past at a great rate. I couldn't see who was inside it because the curtains were all drawn tight just as we had them in our car. And that isn't all."

Rushton detected signs of excitement in Tony's tones, and kept back what he himself had seen until Tony should finish. He merely said:

"What is the rest?"

"I saw Madame Goupolis and the Black Eagle drive past. They were only about ten minutes behind Menes, and it was only a fluke that I saw them, for I was on the point of coming away."

"Good!" said Rushton. "You didn't spot Wu Ling as well, I suppose?"

"No, sir. You don't mean to say he was coming down, too, do

you?"

"He must have, because he is here," answered Rushton. "But it is no fault of yours that you did not spot him, for I have an idea that he came by train. If he fixed up with Menes to come they would not all come by car, even if they did keep the curtains down. Menes is no fool, and he knows we have an army of spies on his trail. If you actually saw the Black Eagle and Madame Goupolis, I take it they were not shy of being seen."

"They were in an open touring car, guv'nor."

"Um! Well, I have not been altogether unsuccessful. I prowled round the waterfront and spotted the yacht Sultan out in the harbour."

"The Sultan! Then Somerton and Fetherston must be along with Pherison."

"It looks like it, and I fancy we might find Mathew Cardolak on board as well. At any rate, there is some sort of meeting taking place on board this evening, for Menes, Wu Ling, Madame Goupolis and the Black Eagle have all gone out."

"Good God! Do you mean to say you have seen the whole bunch and let me go ahead telling you about the cars?"

Rushton laughed quietly, but had no time to reply, for just then there came a knock at the door which led to the back room, and the old native woman entered. She approached Rushton, and in a few whispers told him that food was ready in the back room.

From the fact that she did not keep up the pose which she had first adopted, Rushton gathered that, during the afternoon, she had taken care that no spies should be hanging about, and, indeed, he was right.

They followed her through the low doorway, and there a low table had been piled with simple, but, as they soon discovered, well-cooked native food. A young lad, clad in spotless white garments, was waiting to serve them, and now and then they caught sight of a pretty native girl peeping shyly through the crack of the door as the meal proceeded.

They finished the meal quickly and in silence, for Rushton had plenty to think about and little time to get his plans adjusted.

As soon as they had finished he lit a cigarette and leant back, smoking, and still sunk deep in thought.

And then suddenly he lifted his head and signed for the native boy to come close. When he had done so Rushton whispered to him to go and fetch his grandmother, and the lad disappeared as silently as a shadow.

The old woman came in a few moments later, and for about five minutes she and Rushton carried on an earnest whispered conversation in Arabic. She nodded her head energetically from time to time, and seemed to make suggestions which Rushton seemed to think well of.

Then she turned and gave vent to a sharp hiss, which was evidently a signal for her grandson to come, for he entered almost at once.

He approached them and the old woman gave him detailed instructions of some sort. Then she glanced at Rushton, who nodded, and she took her departure.

When she was gone Rushton signed to Tony and the young detective followed him into the front room.

Then Rushton dragged out the old basket which he had had with him at the Pyramids and which had held his listening-in outfit. Tony closed the door leading to the street, and together they made a careful examination of the apparatus.

Tony didn't know yet just to what purpose Rushton intended using the outfit that evening, but he was an expert hand with that sort of thing, and he soon pronounced it in good working order.

Rushton then replaced it in the basket and rose. He gave a low hiss, such as the old woman had emitted, and the native lad came through from the back room.

He seemed to know just what to do, for he took up the basket and made for the door. Rushton and Tony followed him, and once in the street they set off at a shuffling pace in the direction of the lower town.

On the way Rushton explained briefly to Tony what he proposed doing. It was a daring plan which he outlined, and one in which not only he and Tony, but the native lad as well, would be taking his life in his hands. But the prospect of what was to come made the blood course more quickly through Tony's veins, for he was chafing for action. And before that night was over he was to get all he wanted.

As they descended into the town they could see that the blanket of mist still lay over the harbour. It did not seem to Rushton to have lifted any higher since he looked down upon it before, but it was still as dense, as they discovered when they reached the waterfront.

Once in the thick of the mist there they could only follow their guide.

Both Rushton and Tony possess what is known as a good sense of direction, but had they attempted to find their way through that wall of white fog they would have been in imminent danger of walking into the harbour, and they would not have stood one chance in ten of going through with the plan Rushton had made.

But their native guide went ahead with almost as much certainty as if it were perfectly clear.

Above the mist the moon still shone brightly, but not even its blur was visible to them. The only way they could tell it was there was by the ghostly whiteness of the wet blanket which wrapped them about.

The native lad kept on until he came to the jetty which Rushton had visited before returning to the hut.

He had not spent long there, but his visit had been sufficient to gain him certain information he was after, and when he had told the old woman what he proposed doing, she agreed with him that by the time they reached the waterfront the jetty used by the harbour boatmen would in all probability be quite deserted.

And it seemed as if she were right, for while they came upon scores of empty boats swinging free, there was not a single human being to be seen.

The boy paused some distance along the jetty and looked up at Rushton for instructions. Rushton pointed down at one of the dim shapes in the water beneath.

"Any one of those will do," he said in Arabic. "All we want is a sound craft with two pairs of oars."

"They are all the same, effendi," whispered the lad. "We shall take this one if the effendi pleases." And he pointed down at one a little to the left.

Rushton nodded, and the lad dropped lightly into the boat. Tony followed him, and then came Rushton.

The Arab boy got busy with some rags which he had brought along with him, and in a few minutes he had roughly but effectually muffled all four oars.

Then he untied the painter and took his place in the stern, for the task of steering had been allotted to him.

Rushton had explained to the old woman the exact location of the yacht which he had seen that afternoon. He had marked it against each horn of the harbour as he stood at the boatman's jetty, and from this had given the woman as much of the direction as he could. He also instructed her grandson from this material, and they were now about to see if the lad could guide them out to their objective.

It was their only hope, for neither Rushton nor Tony could ever have found it in that mist. But the lad had been one of the waterfront youngsters for years, and knew every inch of it, as well as every mood of the sea and harbour.

He said that he thought he could find the craft which the effendi was seeking, and Rushton was gambling everything on the possibility that he would be able to make good.

He put Tony at the bow oars, while he himself took the other pair, for he wanted to be where he could whisper to the native lad if necessary. Then at a slow, even stroke they pulled out from the jetty, and a few moments later they were entirely alone in the dense blanket of mist.

Rushton did not attempt to give the lad the direction. He had done all he could in that respect, and now it was up to the boy to smell out the yacht if it could be done.

Tony took his stroke from the pace Rushton set, which was the same slow sweep with which they had started, for while they had a quarter of a mile or so to go, Rushton knew it would be easier for the Arab to judge the distance at a long, steady stroke than if they made a quicker pace.

Besides, every care must be taken to prevent the oars from making any sound.

He could see dimly the figure of the lad in the stern sheets. It was scarcely perceptible whether he was shifting the tiller ropes or not, but Rushton did not interfere.

If he had seen the lad jerking them this way and that way, he would have suspected that he was in a quandary which way to steer.

But he held steadily to the course he had set at the start, and on and on they went into that white world, which seemed just then to be all the universe to them.

Ten minutes passed—a quarter of an hour went by, and still the oars dipped and rose in slow unison.

Rushton figured that more than twenty minutes must have elapsed from the time they had pushed off from the jetty, and he was beginning to think that they must be well out in the harbour, when the

Arab lad leant forward suddenly and made a low sound.

Instantly Rushton rested on his oars, and Tony followed suit. Then the native lad said in a whisper:

"There is a craft just ahead, effendi. I do not know if it is the one we seek or another. We shall drift past and you can see. There is a current here which will take us without the use of the oars."

Rushton turned and tried to penetrate with his eyes the wall of mist beyond, but, peer as he might, he could see absolutely nothing.

He thought the lad must be making a mistake, and was about to say so when suddenly there loomed up a dim, black shape, almost directly in a straight line with the bow of the boat.

He knew then that the eyes of the native lad possessed qualities of sight which were lacking in his own, and he began to feel a little more certainty in the guidance to which they had submitted themselves.

They sat watching while the dim bulk ahead grew nearer and nearer; and then, startlingly, so close did it seem, a voice broke the silence.

It was someone on the deck of the ship ahead, and the words were Italian.

Rushton listened, and then, as they swept past, close in under the stern of the ship, he stood up and tried to make out her name and port of registry. But he could not do so, and, shooting out his hand, caught hold of a loose rope which was dangling over the stern.

The Arab lad had evidently seen his intention, for he dropped the tiller ropes, and before Tony could reach Rushton the native had caught hold of the loose rope and was going up like a monkey.

They could see him dimly, swinging above them, as he clung close to the stern; then he slid down the rope, landing close beside Rushton.

"I know not the way to say the word, effendi," he whispered, "but I have been taught the letters of the effendi's tongue, and can give those which are painted above."

"What are they?" asked Rushton.

"They go 'G-I-U-L-I-O,' effendi. And after that, under the other name is, 'G-E-N-O-A.'"

"Giulio. That is Italian, and, of course, the port of registry is Genoa," muttered Rushton. "Now what ship was lying nearest to the yacht this afternoon. I remember! It was an ugly-looking, green-painted tramp. I wonder if this is the same? If so, we should be only a biscuit-throw away from the yacht, which means that this lad has brought us almost as directly as would have been possible in broad daylight. But we must make sure."

Then he turned to Tony.

"Can you go up the rope? If you can get in close to the hull, try to see what colour it is painted. I have an idea about this craft."

"Sure I can go up," answered Tony, not to be outdone by the agility of a native lad; and forthwith he was scrambling up as quickly and noiselessly as the other. He kept on until he was just a dark blur from below, and then Rushton could see that he was working his way in close to the hull. He seemed to remain motionless for some time, and then he came sliding down. He landed on the seat close to where Rushton was standing, and whispered:

"The hull is painted green, guv'nor—green with a broad white stripe."

Rushton slapped his thigh softly. He had forgotten that white stripe, but now he remembered it, and he knew that the craft against which they were lying was the same tramp he had spotted at anchor near the yacht in the afternoon. He turned to the Arab lad and explained just where they were. Then he pointed off towards the port quarter.

"If the ship we seek is where she was this afternoon, she ought to be just over there," he said. "It would be about fifty metres. Do you think you can find it?"

"If the ship is there, and the effendi will trust me, I shall find it," said the boy simply, and Rushton was satisfied.

They sat down again, and when the Arab lad had once more taken hold of the tiller ropes Tony allowed the boat to drift away from the Italian cargo tramp. She was soon just a fading blur in the mist, and then, at a sign from Rushton, Tony took his oars.

They rowed even more cautiously than ever now, and Rushton could see that the Arab was pulling fairly hard on the right-hand rope.

They seemed to come round in a sort of wide circle, but in reality they were moving in almost a straight line.

The other impression was got because they were in the full sweep of the current which cuts through the very centre of the harbour—no one seems to understand just why.

Then all of a sudden the Arab boy leant forward again, and,

turning, Rushton gazed ahead. As before, he could see nothing at first, but then, with ghostly swiftness, a dark bulk loomed up, and in a lew minutes they were sweeping in close to another ship.

They allowed the boat to run on until they were almost under the stern. As they came round, Tony's groping fingers encountered an anchor chain. He gripped it hard, and after a brief struggle managed to bring the boat right in under the out-thrust of the stern.

To climb here was easier than it had been before, and the Arab lad went up swiftly.

They could just see him clinging to something up above, and then, after a few minutes, he returned. Once again he spelled out the name of the craft to Rushton, and as Rushton heard him say "S-U-L-T-A-N," he knew that they had hit a bullseye where there were a thousand chances to one that they would not do so.

He patted the lad's shoulder in commendation, and, turning to Tony, motioned for him to squat down in the bottom of the boat.

CHAPTER 12.

Rushton had already made tentative plans which depended on the first step which they had just achieved. The idea had come to him during the afternoon when he had sat behind the piles of bales of cotton, watching the yacht.

He figured then that if he could only get out to the craft in some way, he might be able to follow up the line of inquiry which had brought him to Alexandria, and a little later, when he saw the group on the outer jetty, he had striven more than ever to figure out some way of doing so.

He had considered the possibility of going along with Menes' servants and the luggage, but he had soon discarded this.

However, the thing remained in his mind, and while at first the threat of the mist coming in had presented itself as a handicap, he altered his opinion when a new plan took shape in his mind.

But, as he had said, that depended entirely on whether he could get out to the yacht without being spotted; and, thanks to the native "water-sense" of the Arab lad, he had done so.

Now for the next step.

Squatting in the bottom of the boat, he explained to Tony just what had to be done. To employ native lad for this part of the job was out of the question. Only he or Tony could handle it, and, as usual, he left it to Tony to volunteer to do so.

Tony jumped at the chance of action, though Rushton impressed upon him strongly the need for the utmost caution. If that mob of renegades was still on board, as he believed, then they were, metaphorically speaking, sitting right on top of a case of dynamite.

Tony listened to his instructions with silent attention. Then when Rushton had finished, he picked up the microphone and the crimped receiver and attached the one to the other with utmost care. Next he affixed the end of the wire, and unwound enough to give it free play while he went up the side.

Rushton had made a close study of the stern quarters of the yacht from the shore. Not that he really needed to do so, for he had seen the Sultan on several occasions, and he knew the layout of the ship as well as if he had cruised in her.

But he was leaving nothing to chance, and he was able to explain to Tony just which ports opened into the main saloon, and which ones to avoid where they served private cabins.

Of course, Rushton knew that it was quite possible that whatever the meeting was being held for had long ago been settled. On the other hand, he figured that it was also quite possible that business would not be discussed until after dinner.

This was no bar-parlour meeting of ordinary crooks. It was a conference between some of the most powerful criminals at large, but the personnel which Rushton had already seen was sufficient to tell him that something of a gigantic nature must be afoot.

Therefore, haste would be out of place. If they were too late, then the only thing to be done would be to make back for the shore and figure out some new plan.

When Tony had attached the crimped receiver to his shirt (he had removed the upper cotton garment which he had been wearing, as well as the white cotton cloth about his lower limbs, and was now clad only in a loin cloth and shirt) by a hook at the top of the apparatus, he caught hold of the nearest chain, and began to climb.

His progress this time was much slower than it had been before, for he had to take care that the microphone did not bump against the side and suffer damage.

Rushton watched him anxiously as the blur of his body grew dimmer and dimmer, and then it almost disappeared from view as Tony worked his way round the curve of the stern in search of the nearest port which would look into the cabin.

Rushton was hoping that at least one of the ports would be open. The yacht was, he knew, equipped with electric fans, whilst the mist had made the night cooler than ordinary. But, even so, the atmosphere was close and heavy, and it would have been natural for the ports in the main saloon to be open on the shore side, which was the side along which Tony was working.

Rushton paid out the wire slowly and gently as he felt it begin to tauten as Tony moved along; then at last it remained slack in his hand, although he could feel it quivering constantly as the lad worked in some way with it at the other end.

Then all movement ceased, and there was dead silence for the space of perhaps half a minute.

Rushton was looking upwards anxiously. If all were well with Tony, then the blur of his body should be showing soon. If not, then it must mean that something had gone wrong, though it did not seem possible that the lad would allow himself to be "jumped" without shouting out some sort of warning to his chief.

Then Rushton heaved an audible sigh of relief as he caught sight of a blurred shadow coming along high above from the direction which Tony had taken. He and the Arab lad stood tensely while it grew plainer and plainer, and then began to descend. Half a minute later Tony dropped silently into the boat beside them.

"Right as rain, guv'nor!" he whispered. "The very first open port was one of the saloon ports. I had a look through, and the whole bunch is in there at a long table—old Mathew Cardolak at one end, Menes at the other, Wu Ling on Cardolak's right, and Brady on his left."

"Brady!" jerked Rushton. "I did not know he was here."

"He must have arrived before or after the others. Anyway, he is there, guv'nor, as well as the Black Eagle, on Menes' right, and the Greek woman on his left. Then, the Three Musketeers are all there as well. It is a gathering of the clans all right."

"What about the microphone?" asked Rushton.

"I think it will pick up what they say. I hung it by the hook to the rim of the porthole frame. That would be invisible from inside the saloon. But I had to work as silently as I could. They were too much interested in something Menes was saying to notice me during the second or so I was at the port, but I could hear someone on the deck just above me. If it hadn't been for the mist he would have spotted me, sure. As it is, I don't think he heard a thing."

"Good man! We shall soon see if the microphone works."

With that Rushton stepped over the seat and again squatted down near the basket in which he had brought the apparatus.

He took up the little black box, which he had concealed in the sand beneath his ear when he was feigning sleep at the bottom of the small pyramid the previous evening—how far away and long ago that seemed to him just then!—and brought it into position.

At first he heard nothing but a sort of low, buzzing sound; but as he shifted a small vulcanite knob back and forth he suddenly caught a voice clear and distinct, and he held the adjustment at that.

Then he settled back to listen, and for almost a quarter of an hour he remained as motionless as the Sphinx itself, while there came over that wire everything that was being said in the saloon as clearly almost as if he, too, were at that table of intrigue!

And never in all his career had Grant Rushton listened to

anything more condemning than in those minutes in the white mist. A good deal must have gone before, as he could tell from what he first heard, but not all.

They had arrived some time after the conference had opened, but it was still in full swing, and from what he did pick up, it was not difficult to guess as to what had been said already. For certain references were made from time to time which gave him a clue.

The conference was by no means over when he removed the black box from his ear; but for the present Rushton had heard enough. What was now going on was a discussion of ways and means.

What Rushton had got hold of was the real meat of the thing, with sufficient particulars to give him something really definite to work on, and enough evidence to implicate every man-jack— and the woman, there.

He had looked for something big, something epochal in the criminal world; but he did not dream he would get hold of the sort of thing he had heard discussed.

It was not the discussion of a big criminal coup to which he had "listened-in."

It was something very different and far more comprehensive.

It was the blending of crime and politics dished out to satisfy the greed of the diverse desires of each one there.

It was Menes who did most of the talking, but now and then Rushton had been able to distinguish other voices—that of Wu Ling on one occasion; Brady two or three times, the Greek woman often; the Black Eagle once, he thought, and Pherison for the Three Musketeers.

The only person at the table, according to Tony's catalogue, whose voice he had not heard was Mathew Cardolak.

He had listened to a phrase now and then addressed directly to the multi-millionaire, and from what followed Rushton knew he must have made answer in some way. But it must have been with a gesture or a simple nod of the head, which was not unusual, for Rushton knew how sparing the old man was with his words at any time.

But the fact remained that he had heard, with his own ears, sufficient to condemn every person there.

And yet he could not get at them by ordinary process of law.

Egypt was now an independent country, and the yacht was lying in Egyptian territorial waters.

Of course, Rushton could lay before the Secret Service of his own country just what he had overheard and that department in turn, could make revelations to the Egyptian Government.

It would be difficult, however, for the Egyptian Government to make a move without irrefutable proof. Menes was too great a power in Egypt to be tackled otherwise.

He could simply deny that any such conference had taken place, or that he had ever discussed such things as he was accused of. In other words he could simply laugh at Rushton and wait for a better opportunity to come.

Brady would soon be able to lose himself in the desert, for he had the whole stretch of North Africa to choose from, and that gave him thousands of square miles in which to roam.

Mathew Cardolak and the Three Musketeers would be perfectly safe while they remained out of British territorial waters, and there was nothing on which Rushton could hold the Black Eagle or Goupolis.

As for Wu Ling that wily celestial would be able to take care of himself. And with each one denying flatly that Rushton's statement was correct, what could he do. Only those who have struggled against departmental red tape can appreciate the problem which he was facing.

He had been sent out to get evidence in such a way that no subterfuge of the guilty persons would avail them.

In other words, those whom he was seeking to catch must be caught red-handed, and he was a long way yet from accomplishing that.

But he had achieved something, and now he was anxious to get back to Cairo as soon as possible and talk over with Lawrence Malone, and certain other persons, in official positions, just what he had discovered.

Therefore, while he would have been interested enough in the rest of the conversation that was taking place in the saloon of the yacht, caution told him to get away while he could.

He bent close to Tony and told him what he had planned. The lad started upwards again almost at once, and soon he was again just an indeterminate blur above them.

Then he disappeared round the curve of the stern, and Rushton and the Arab lad stood gazing up towards where they had last seen him, waiting for him to reappear with the microphone. A half-minute passed; a full minute went by. Then suddenly, and with the violence of a pistol-shot, a single sharp, warning cry came down through the mist.

It needed no more than that to tell Rushton that Tony had been discovered.

Rushton caught hold of the chain and made ready to go up. After that first cry dead silence fell, and for the beat of thirty seconds it lasted.

Then pandemonium seemed to break loose above. There were shouts, cries, curses, and bumpings, and with a smothered curse Rushton began to climb.

He was up less than two feet when a pistol cracked, and then he felt the Arab lad dragging at his legs. He slipped and landed in the bottom of the boat.

He turned savagely on the boy, but the latter still clung to him and kept pointing round towards the starboard side of the yacht.

Rushton at last gathered what he was trying to tell him, and in a flash he saw that the boy's plan was better than his own.

He made a gesture of assent, and the lad sprang to the painter which had been wrapped round the chain. He loosened it, and together they began to push the boat round the stern, Rushton using one hand for that purpose and another to get his automatic out.

As they rounded the stern the full force of the shouting above caught them, and then a brilliant light began stabbing through the heavy mist. Someone had turned on a searchlight.

A pistol crashed out again, its sound hammered down upon them by the heavy mist-laden air, and then Rushton heard Tony's voice raised again in a shrill, high cry—not a cry of fear, but one, he knew, of warning to him.

Whatever was happening to him, he was determined that Rushton should get away if he could. But Rushton's intentions were very different. He knew what Tony's fate would be if he fell into the hands of that murderous gang above and his identity were discovered.

And he knew, equally, what it would be even if they thought him but a spying native lad. Menes would tolerate nothing like that.

Then suddenly something struck against Rushton's leg, and the next instant the black box and the wire which was attached to it were jerked overboard.

Almost at the same moment there came another cry from above, this time not in Tony's voice, and something hurtled down into the water just in front of them.

By this time the person operating the searchlight had got it focussed in a straight line down the side of the yacht, and while it did not light the scene clearly, it was sufficient to show up the boat and its two occupants, and a struggling mass in the water ahead.

Rushton did not need to ask whether Tony was one of that pair or not. His instinct told him the lad was there, and he was just turning to tell the Arab lad to take to his own safety before going over the side to Tony's assistance, when something else hurtled down from above and struck the bottom of the boat with terrific force.

It hit as if it were a great iron weight, but whatever missile had been used, it had luckily missed both Rushton and the lad.

The bottom of the boat was not strong enough to withstand the shock, for the weight went clean through it, and the next second the water came rushing through and into the boat, through a hole fully a foot in diameter.

Willy-nilly, there was no choice but to go over the side, and they took to the water just as a fusillade of bullets struck where they had been a second before.

Rushton had no chance then to look to the Arab lad.

His one concern was for the safety of Tony, and now he blessed the foresight that had caused him to strip to the loincloth, as had Tony and the native lad.

He made for the struggling pair ahead with a quick overhand stroke.

Several bullets struck the water close to him, miraculously none hit him, and before the marksman could improve on his aim, Rushton was close to the struggling pair.

The searchlight had now been swung round, and Rushton was able to see for certain that Tony was there. He could see, too, that he was locked in a life and death struggle with a negro—one of the crew of the yacht, he supposed.

As a matter of fact he was right. He had guessed pretty well what had happened. On his second trip round the cabin porthole Tony had reached his goal in safety.

He had clung there trying to unhook the microphone to bring back with him when, without the slightest warning, someone had dropped down over the rail close beside him.

A voice had shot a question at him, and then, as a heavy hand reached for his throat, Tony had given vent to the shrill cry of warning which Rushton had heard.

Clinging with one hand he had tried to drag his assailant away so that he could force him into the water, but the big black nigger who had tackled him was an old hand at that game, and in less than a minute Tony knew that he hadn't a chance.

It was then that he had uttered his second cry of warning, and by then several persons on deck had been brought to the scene by the racket.

Tony did not know it, but the whole crowd in the saloon were rushing up on deck, and it was Algy Somerton who got the searchlight working.

But Tony was resolved that, at any cost, they should not discover that a microphone had been in use to spy upon them. He concentrated every effort on jerking the thing free, and it was then, just as he succeeded in doing so, the negro got his hand down and forced him to drop.

That was when the fall dragged the box, with its wire attached, out of the boat, and the whole apparatus sank to the bottom.

Then Tony set himself to break free from the brute who was trying to throttle his life out. He knew he could never overpower the negro, and that his only chance was to get clear and swim for it.

If he could strike a faster pace than the other he had a chance of getting away in the mist, but if not he knew that he could count the remainder of his existence in seconds.

And it was just then that Grant Rushton reached the pair.

Rushton was more than savage. What he had heard uttered by those criminals and renegades filled him with a cold rage at the thought that any man who had once known British birth and once walked a free man in England, could be so far lost to all pride of birth and country as to mix it as they were mixing it with spawn of the East like Menes and Wu Ling.

Flash Brady, and more particularly the Three Musketeers, were in his mind then. For Mathew Cardolak he had nothing but contempt, and the case of the Black Eagle was different.

But these others—the thought of it all sickened him and filled his soul with loathing, and there was something of that surging up in him when he saw the hands of the brutal black beast at Tony's throat.

Rushton struck the struggling pair with the force of a porpoise travelling at high speed. The shock was terrific, and the nigger gave vent to a grunt as Rushton hit him.

They might shoot with every weapon they possessed for all it entered Rushton's mind in that moment. He was filled utterly with one idea, and one idea only, and that was to throttle that black beast as he was throttling Tony.

He knew there was no time for finesse. It was a case of brute strength against brute strength, and when it was necessary Grant Rushton could operate with the gloves off and all rules discarded.

He went at it just like that now. He got one knee up against the small of the negro's back, and, bracing hard there, hit him one, two; one, two, just back of the ear, and in those blows he put every ounce of strength he could muster in such an awkward position.

He got his first result when the black released his hold on Tony's throat. Rushton could not see that the lad instantly went under, for his senses had all but left him. And he was only dimly aware that someone had surged past him and caught hold of Tony.

The spirit of the men who served with the colours was showing in that Arab lad just then for, instead of seeking his own safety, the Arab had hung about treading water and watching his chance to help the two persons for whom he was ready to give his life.

And there was a particularly fine point to courage of that sort when it is remembered that, just above him, was Menes, the most-to-be-feared man in all Egypt, and one to whom the life of the little Arab lad would have meant less than the brief existence of a fly!

No, Rushton saw none of that. He was too occupied in hammering the killer black, and now the negro knew that death was clinging to his shoulders, for he clawed with a wild and frantic desperation to get away. But he might as well have tried to tear loose the iron plates from the side of the yacht.

He tore the flesh from Rushton's knuckles; he twisted like a madman; he tried to scream, he tried to kick, and if his tongue hadn't been protruding from between his thickening lips he would have tried to bite.

But that incubus behind him never shifted. He clung worse than any old man of the sea, and so interested were those on deck in the course of the terrible struggle between what they took to be one of the crew and a native from the shore, that they had let up on the shooting.

Tony and the Arab lad had been forgotten, too, for the moment, and assisted by the latter, Tony had managed to swim away a little distance.

Then at last Rushton felt the first quiver that told him what was happening. He knew his man was giving in, and like a flash he followed up his advantage.

His right fist came back once more, and again he struck. It was that blow that did the trick. As the black suddenly collapsed like a limp sack, Rushton jerked away his hands and drove the body forward with all the force of his knee. He took one look above, then he turned and began swimming at top speed.

He was unable to see what had become of Tony or the Arab lad; but as he dashed on through the water the native lad called to him, and, guided by his voice, Rushton changed his direction.

By now those on deck seemed to realise what was happening, and that the terrible struggle they had been watching was no mere battle between a shore native and one of the crew of the yacht.

They could not understand just what it was all about, and the evidence of the boat and the listening-in apparatus had both disappeared beneath the surface.

But some of them at least thought it was good enough to prevent the three in the water escaping and the fusillade opened again.

A voice was raised, too, yelling an order for a boat to be lowered; but before a hit could be registered or the boat got into the water, Rushton had rejoined the two lads, and they pushed on until even the powerful rays of the searchlight failed to pick them out through the mist.

Rushton's first care was to find out how Tony was faring. The lad protested that he would be all right soon, and that he could swim if they took it slowly.

It was here that the Arab lad broke in, speaking eagerly, as he told Rushton that if they just let themselves go with the current they must fetch up eventually on the beach near the eastern horn of the harbour.

Rushton knew that the boat from the yacht would scour every available bit of water as long as they could keep within hail of the yacht, and, as their best chance lay in getting outside that radius, he figured that no plan could be better than the native boy suggested.

So they turned, and, swimming easily, let the outward current carry them whither it would.

Rushton thought in his own mind that they stood a pretty good chance of being taken out to sea, but he was willing to trust to the boy's knowledge of the vagaries of the currents in the harbour after his feat of finding the yacht in that dense fog.

It was impossible to judge the passage of time, but it seemed well over an hour that they had been swimming on and on, and quite twenty minutes since the cries of those who were searching for them had died away that the Arab lad spoke and touched Rushton's arm.

"I can hear the water on the beach, just here to the right, effendi," he said. "A few metres now and we shall make it."

Rushton and Tony turned obediently, and in less than a minute they saw a dull, black line ahead of them. Two minutes later they were in shallow water and wading ashore. They landed on what seemed to be a deserted bit of beach, and Rushton hadn't the remotest notion just where it could be. But the native lad went ahead unhesitatingly, and the two Britishers followed him.

They crossed a sandy track of sorts, and seemed to climb for quite a distance.

Then suddenly, without the slightest warning that the mist was thinning, they burst through the white blanket into the bright light of the moon that was almost full, and, with the upper portion of their bodies protruding from the fog, they stood gazing across the misty sea at the twinkling lights in the higher part of Alexandria.

CHAPTER 13.

Grant Rushton had, as he told Tony, heard enough of the conversation which took place in the saloon on board the Sultan to appal him. But he had not heard all. Nor did he know of the various currents of greed and ambition which were at work among that motley company.

Menes' purpose was sufficiently well known to Rushton for him to guess pretty nearly just what was at the back of the Egyptian's mind in the new outrage which was being planned.

Nor was it very difficult for him to guess what bait would induce Mathew Cardolak to lend part of his colossal wealth and himself to this plot.

As for the Three Musketeers, they would follow Cardolak, for the multi-millionaire meant their bread-and-butter, while Menes' protection meant their present safety.

Menes might be powerful, but the activities of the White Flag Society could not be carried on without money, and, while Rushton knew enormous sums had already been spent, he knew, too, that the exchequer of the society was not inexhaustible.

Menes was wealthy enough in his own right, and had, of course, put a great fortune into the society in the past. But a recruit like Mathew Cardolak would be an enormous asset, and Menes was no fool.

As to just what was at the back of the mind of the Black Eagle, Rushton could not fathom. While not rich, he had, by his own showing, sufficient to live on comfortably, and it was just a little difficult to figure how he expected to benefit from his alliance with the others unless he was after money or power.

On one occasion he had stated to Grant Rushton that it was his intention to devote the rest of his life to the professional practice of criminal deeds, and this, Rushton thought, might explain how he had drifted into the gang. He did not think for a single moment that the Black Eagle was infatuated with the Greek woman.

The position of Flash Brady—or Sakr-el-Droog, as he chose now to be called—was easier of understanding. Rushton knew all about the game Brady had been playing in Morocco, and he knew that the ex-inspector from Scotland Yard was still consumed by the same overwhelming ambition which had been the cause of his original downfall.

Now it was not only wealth, but power as well that was urging him on, and while Rushton knew the whole colossal business could and must end in one way—failure—he knew that a vast deal of damage would be done, and a great number of lives would be lost before the finish unless their plans were nipped in the bud.

As for Wu Ling he had heard what the Chinaman had said at the meeting in answer to the proposals that Menes had made. Wu Ling might or might not be on the level with Menes. No one could tell that for the celestial was unfathomable, and, if it suited his purposes, he would double-cross the Egyptian as coolly and as bloodlessly as he would crack an eggshell.

Madame Goupolis was simply a professional spy, and her price was what the highest bidder would pay if he could overcome her fear of Menes and the White Flag Society.

Rushton knew exactly where to place her.

It was on these various phases of the matter he was pondering as the Arab lad guided him and Tony back to the disreputable quarter of the city where they had taken up temporary lodging. And the result of his cogitations was that he decided to return to Cairo without delay.

From what he had overheard he knew that it was Menes' intention to do the same. He did not know what the Greek woman would do next, but he had heard sufficient to tell him that most of the gang would be on board the Sultan when she sailed.

But that was not worrying Rushton just then, for, if he could depend on his own hearing, then he knew it would not be very long before the yacht returned. And in her would be those who sailed away.

It was impossible for him to handle both ends of the thing at the same time. His only hope was to anticipate their intention, and plan to outwit them. To do that his next step must be taken in Cairo.

As soon as they were back at the hut he sent the Arab boy off with an urgent message to one of the Secret Service agents in Alexandria.

This was simply a general instruction that the yacht Sultan, then in harbour, should be closely watched, and the movements of all persons coming ashore from her shadowed.

As soon as there might be anything to report a code telegram was to be sent to Lawrence Malone at Cairo.

He also sent word for the car which had brought him to Alexandria to be on the outskirts of the beggars' quarters as quickly as could be arranged, to run back to Cairo, and the old woman's granddaughter was sent off to keep watch for this.

Thus it was that he and Tony got away about an hour later.

Rushton would have preferred reaching his destination during the hours of the night, but he knew that could not be managed, so he had to trust to luck that he and Tony would be able to slip out of the car somewhere along the Meni House Road without being seen.

As a matter of fact they sped along the Meni House Road during the hot hours of mid-morning, and, by a little manoeuvring they got to the "Thieves' Hut" in what Rushton thought was safety.

There they lay doggo for the whole day. With what food they had saved from the hamper which Malone had sent along with them, and the dates Rushton had left behind, they were able to make two frugal repasts, and as there was plenty of water in the hut they didn't do so badly.

But Rushton was anxious for the night to come. He had sent a message to Malone that he wished to see him urgently, and he knew the Secret Service man would come the very first moment it was safe.

Then, too, he was hoping that Malone would have had some sort of message from the agents in Alexandria regarding the movements of the yacht, and some, at least, of those aboard her.

By nine o'clock he was beginning to get impatient, and a score of times or more he sent Tony scouting to see if there were any signs of Malone.

Each time the young detective had come back with a negative answer; but, a few minutes past nine, when he stole out again, he returned stealthily, to report that there was a figure coming towards the hut from the direction of the Meni House Road.

They crouched in the corner and watched the irregular oblong of the window.

Presently there was a shadow, then a bulky silhouette, and, just as two nights before, the opening was almost filled by someone who was standing just outside. There was a slight sound, and next they could see the other person coming in over the sill.

Still they waited, and it was not until the intruder was well inside that Rushton switched on his electric torch. They both breathed a sigh of relief as they saw that the heavily burnoused figure was indeed Lawrence Malone.

Rushton switched out the torch at once, and they waited until

Malone came across to the corner where they were crouching. He sank beside them with a faint rustling sound, and then his whisper broke the stillness.

"I came as soon as I could, Rushton. There was an official dinner which I had to attend. But, after all, it was just as well, for just before I came away I received another code message from Alexandria."

"Another? Do you mean you have had more than one?"

"Yes, I had the first one this afternoon. From the contents I gathered it was in connection with your visit there, but it is all Greek to me—meaning no pun, although it does mention the Greek woman, Madame Goupolis."

"What did they say?" asked Rushton in an eager whisper.

"I brought copies of them, but I can tell you the gist of them, so it won't be necessary to switch on the light. The first says that the yacht Sultan cleared from Alexandria for Tangier this morning."

"Ah! I expected that. And the other?"

Malone leant forward, so there would be not the slightest possibility of his voice carrying beyond the ears of Rushton and Tony.

"The other," he breathed, "said that Menes, Madame Goupolis, and a Chinaman had left by motor-car for Cairo this afternoon. Also, that an Arab sheik, who had also come ashore from the yacht, had made a few purchases in the city, and had then left in a separate car for Cairo. He got away about half an hour after the others."

"Excellent!" murmured Rushton. "That agent down there deserves commendation for this bit of work, Malone."

"What is it all about, Rushton? What have you discovered at Alexandria?"

"I, with Tony's assistance, have unearthed the most colossal plot this White Flag gang out here has ever conceived," whispered Rushton in reply. "Not only is it the biggest thing by far that the scoundrelly Menes has attempted, but he has secured the assistance of about the choicest bunch of rascals out of gaol. Listen and I will tell you, Malone.

"From what you yourself know and have gathered from our conversations, you need no telling as to the identity of the mystery multimillionaire, Mathew Cardolak, who, although he lives in the United States, is always intriguing out in the Near East.

"You know also of the three desperate criminals who work under his segis—the Three Musketeers. They have sought sanctuary in

Egypt more than once."

"I know them—all."

"And Flash Brady of whom I have told you; of the man known as the Black Eagle, who is at Shepheard's, where the Goupolis woman is staying; and of Wu Ling whom we were discussing last night. Well, Malone, to use Tony's words, there was a regular gathering of the clans on board the Sultan last night. I know, for Tony and I were present for part of the time, and overheard enough to condemn the lot."

Only long years and training and working where a false move meant instant death enabled Lawrence Malone to suppress the exclamation that rose to his lips.

"You and Tony were present?" he whispered, sharply. "What do you mean?"

Forthwith Rushton related in detail just what their movements had been from the time they had slipped out of the "Thieves' Hut" the previous night until under cover of the mist they had succeeded in getting alongside the Sultan at the very time that the meeting of the conspirators was in progress. Then:

"And what I heard is more than we have been expecting to find. There are several plots afoot, each one dovetailing into the other, but the *piece de resistance* of the whole thing is nothing less than to bring things to a grand finale by blowing up the Suez Canal, and a goodly number of ships between Port Said and Suez."

"My good heavens."

"Yes," proceeded Rushton, "just that. And, roughly this is the whole lovely scheme. As you know, Flash Brady has been for some time in the Riff. He must have earned the position by some actual worth as a fighter, for the Riffians are pretty hot stuff, and they don't christen a man what they christened Brady unless he deserves it. They call him Sakr-el-Droog, which roughly means Hawk of the Peak, as you know.

"Well, Malone, when I discovered the night before last that Flash Brady was here secretly, I knew he had not come two thousand miles just to look at the desert sand of Egypt or the Pyramids. I knew he must have some plot afoot, and I was certain of it when I saw him speaking with the Goupolis and the Black Eagle. And that told me, too, that it had something to do with the schemes of Menes and the White Flag Society, or, in other words, the murder gang.

90

"And I was right. It would seem that since he has felt the taste of power in the Riff, he wants more of the same thing. It was that same kink in him which ruined him in the start. But this is big, really big. It is nothing less than a linking up of all the races from the Nile to the Atlantic, right across the top of Africa, with a North African black empire as the ultimate goal, and all the northern European races pushed back across the Mediterranean.

"From what I heard Brady is acting as emissary between the native leaders and Menes, and on his way here he had certain interviews in the other countries—Algeria, Tunis, and Tripoli. It is a plot worthy of Napoleon, in a way. But that is only one phase of it. I shall give you more details at another time.

"That explains what Flash Brady was doing on board the Sultan yesterday. Now for our old friend, Wu Ling. Of course, you and I know that it was Wu Ling who was the real power behind Sun-Yat-Sen, the so-called President of the Republic of South China. Sun-Yat-Sen was supposed to hold Canton in the hollow of his hand —so he did, but he held it for Wu Ling. Then Sun-Yat-Sen went very suddenly to Japan.

"The papers had rumours that he was there to try to fix up some sort of a working alliance between the south and the north. But we know different, and we know that he died in Japan very suddenly. I fancy Wu Ling would tell us a good deal about that if the yellow idol could be made to speak. At any rate, I am convinced that Wu Ling suspected Sun-Yat-Sen of playing him false, and simply got rid of him in the good old Chinese way.

"At any rate, Wu Ling, from what I heard, has been dickering with Menes. He is anxious for a rising in China against the white races, at the same time the big effort is made in this part of the world. He wants another rising to take place in India at the same time, and while every European country would be affected to greater or less extent, it is Britain and the British Empire that would feel the brunt of the blows, and whose very existence would be threatened. That is what he is doing in the mix-up, and the price of his assistance to Menes is that it shall all be brought in under one vast scheme.

"As for Mathew Cardolak, he is putting up a big bunch of money—or has agreed to—on the understanding that Menes shall guarantee that he is given certain very valuable excavation rights among the old tombs of Egypt. You know Cardolak would sell his soul for a chance like that. And this is what the murderous bunch of renegades and crooks were discussing on the yacht last evening. And, as I said, the *piece de resistance* of the whole thing is the plot to blow up the Suez Canal, and at the same time destroy as many ships as possible between Port Said and Suez. That, in fact, is planned as the first outrage to signal the new push against us."

"I don't understand how you and Tony ever managed to get away after discovering that," whispered Malone; "but if you had been caught, the first outrage would have been the cutting to pieces of both of you."

"Well, they nearly did catch us at that," responded Rushton. "But a miss is as good as a mile, and we have turned the first trick. But there is not too much time in which to work, Malone. The yacht has cleared ostensibly for Tangier. That is only a blind. She is bound for the Riff to pick up a cargo of a new type of mine which Brady has evolved. I am surprised, in a way, that he didn't go along with them; but I suppose he is remaining here on the ground to keep in touch with Menes and to collect his cash—for, be sure that whatever the plans may be, one dead certainty is that Flash Brady shall get his slice of money in cold cash. I think we can figure on about two weeks."

"Um! As you say, not too much time. But this is a ghastly plot, Rushton. It must be stopped."

"And it is going to be," returned Rushton quietly. "There is not the slightest use, in my opinion, of putting it up officially."

"Not a chance in a million. By the time it got through the web of red tape the whole show would be over."

"That is just what I thought. And that leaves only one way to handle it."

"You mean?"

"We must tackle those hounds and beat them ourselves. I haven't figured out a definite plan yet, but this is how the position stands: The yacht is on her way to the coast of the Riff to load up with mines. She is a very fast craft but she can't get there, load up and get back before a couple of weeks have passed. I have a hunch that I am right about that. At any rate, there was a talk about it, and I fancy that is what was finally decided upon.

"Very well, we know that Cardolak and the Three Musketeers are on board. That locates them for us, and if your report is correct then it would seem that the Black Eagle has also gone along. Menes, Wu

Ling and Madame Goupolis all returned to Cairo together. That means they are in Cairo now. It looks as if Brady has also come this way, but I don't believe he is in Cairo."

"Where do you think he will be hanging out?"

"Well, he came out of the desert the other night when he spoke with the Greek woman and the Black Eagle, and he returned that way. I know that part of the desert pretty well, and I have a hunch that he may be lying low at the oasis of El Adid, which is about thirty-six miles to the west. It is a very small oasis with only a handful of people living there, and tourists never find it out. The next one is in a different direction and much farther off, and that is why I think Brady might be at El Adid. It would just fit in nicely for him, and the thirty-six miles there and back on a good Arab horse would mean nothing to a man who was hardened to the desert."

"By ginger, Rushton, but I believe you are right. We can find out, at any rate."

"That is going to be my job," responded Rushton, quietly. "You are going to have your hands full in Cairo. A constant surveillance of Menes and Wu Ling must be kept. Then Tony is going to have his hands full at the hotel, keeping track of the Greek woman. I shall handle Brady, and it is well that we should settle every possible point to-night, for I start for that oasis before morning."

And Lawrence Malone knew that it would be not the slightest use to argue.

They talked then in cautious whispers for the better part of two hours.

Then Malone rose and stood guard by the window while Rushton gave Tony some last instructions.

The lad was rebelling inwardly that he was not to be allowed to go along with Rushton to El Adid; but orders were orders and he dared not voice a protest.

He listened carefully to what Rushton had to say, and then at a word he went off with Malone, who was to drop him near the hotel.

Each of those three was carrying on his shoulders a load of responsibility that could scarcely have been greater. And each one knew it.

Thus it was that the old beggar man of the Thieves' Hut on the Meni House Road stole across the desert while the moonlight still lay over the limitless sands; stole past the three Pyramids that have stood sentinel there for so many thousands of years, past the brooding Sphinx that might tell so much if it could or would but speak, and then on into the west in the direction of the little and almost unknown oasis of El Adid.

CHAPTER 14.

Tony made his entry into his room at Shepheard's as unobtrusively as he had left it.

Mossop, as usual, was just where he was needed just when he should have been, and, indeed, for the past thirty-six hours he had been on the lookout for his charge. He saw the stealthy figure come creeping across the garden at about midnight, and before Tony was beneath the balcony the cord-ladder was hanging down.

Tony came up with the agility of a cat burglar and lost no time in getting out of his native garments and into a hot bath. Then he slipped on a thin silk dressing-gown and stretched out into a low wicker-chair, while Mossop hovered in attendance.

As a matter of fact, the man was eager for some news as to where Tony had been and what had happened; but Tony did not intend to enlighten him until he heard what had transpired at the hotel during his absence. That was soon told.

"There was not much difficulty," said Mossop in answer to his question. "The young people with whom you have been friendly asked after you, and I just said you were not very well and were keeping to your room. But after the first day they wanted to come up and see you, and as I was afraid they would discover you were not here, I thought it best to say that you had motored out of Cairo to see an English doctor who had his villa a few miles out. I also told them that you might decide to stay there for a few days if he thought he would like to make a thorough examination of you. It was a lie, sir; but, under the circumstances, with so much at stake, I thought I was justified in leading even your friends astray."

"Quite right, Mossop," answered Tony. "It is unfortunate I did not know sooner that I would be going off so abruptly, but it couldn't be helped. And, as you say, this thing is so big that anything is justified as long as it defeats the enemies we are fighting. I have been to Alexandria."

"Alexandria? I wish I could have gone with you."

"I should have been glad to have you, Mossop, but it couldn't be done. The guv'nor and I went off very secretly, and we struck a big thing down there."

"You have seen the chief, then?"

"Yes. I left him to-night. We got back to Cairo early this morning, but have been lying low out on the Meni House Road until we saw

Mr. Malone. The guv'nor has gone off again, but I do not know how long he will be away, or when I shall hear from him again. But we have got to be ready for a summons at any moment. We have struck something real at last, and things are going to begin to bump pretty soon, Mossop, I give you my word."

"I am glad to hear that. I should just like a good crack at some of these people."

"You'll get it," rejoined Tony. "Anything else to report here in Cairo?"

"No. Except that the Greek woman has been away and also the man you call the Black Eagle. But I take it you know about that."

"Yes, I do. Got back to-day, didn't they?"

"Yes!"

"What is the gossip about the town of the attempted murder of Mr. Lushington? Mr. Malone told the guv'nor about it this evening and said that everything went exactly according to plan."

"Well, of course, there is a lot of talk, and from what I can gather it is thought that one of the conspirators must have betrayed his companions. They were caught in the very act, just as they were about to shoot."

Tony chuckled.

"They betrayed themselves but they don't know it—and won't," he said. "That was a smart piece of work on the part of the guv'nor, Mossop, and he pulled off a smarter bit down in Alexandria. We actually overheard the conspirators talking over their plot. Have a look round, and I'll tell you who are in it and what they are planning."

"That will wait, I think, for a little."

At the sound of the voice, Mossop jumped and Tony jerked his head round just as the door of the adjoining bathroom, which had been ajar, was swung open and a man stepped out into the bedroom.

One look and they recognised the Black Eagle —the Black Eagle in full evening dress and with a heavy automatic pistol held loosely in one hand.

"Yes—that will wait for a little, I think," he repeated. "You," and he waved the barrel in Mossop's direction, "get over there behind that chair where Tony is seated. Get your hands up on the back of it and keep them well in sight, for it you try any hanky-panky I shall not hesitate to shoot. And you, my young bucko," he went on, addressing Tony, "sit just as you are, and see that you, too, keep your hands in sight."

He reached behind him and closed the door of the bathroom. Then he leant against the wall and with one hand extracted a cigarette from his case and lit it.

"You reached here a little sooner than I counted on," he went on, when he had taken a few whiffs. "I knew your man was on duty, but I must say you got into the place without me seeing you. But it is sufficient that you are here. You are looking a little more comfortable than when I saw you last night in the water at Alexandria."

Some instinct had told Tony that the Black Eagle was going to mention that.

For the moment the dread killer had appeared, his mind had been working fast to try and figure what had inspired the visit and just before the intruder mentioned Alexandria Tony got a hunch that in some way, they either knew or suspected that he had been one of those in the boat beside the yacht the previous evening while the conference was in progress.

It was that single moment's advantage that enabled him to return a blank stare to the glittering orbs of the Black Eagle.

"I am not going to say I don't know you, for I do," he said, with a self-possession that even Rushton would have admired, and accompanied his words by a fit of the sort of coughing which he had exhibited about the hotel ever since his first coming. "I have seen you about the place for some days, and I know the woman in whose company you have been. But I fail to see what that fact has to do with you invading the privacy of my apartment. If this is a hold-up and you want money, I fancy you are going to be disappointed, for I have very little here. If that isn't the reason, then I'm hanged if I can figure out what all the melodrama is about."

The Black Eagle smiled a cold smile which Tony had seen on one other occasion and which at that time, had been followed by a swift killing.

"Not bad," said the man, "not bad at all. Quite a promising pupil of your master. But that sort of thing won't go down with me. I remarked that you look more comfortable at the present moment than when you were in the water at Alexandria last night."

"And I say that you must be crazy for you are certainly talking through your roof," rejoined Tony spiritedly. "If that is all you have come to say then I don't mind how soon you clear out."

"I'll take that cockiness out of you before I finish with you," said the Black Eagle. "You may think that you have fooled everyone in the hotel that you have been ill in your room for the past few days, but I know better. I know that you left here three nights ago, and that you returned only to-night. You had pretty good cover under the mist last night, but I suspected at the time there was something deeper behind the prowling about the yacht than just three natives trying to steal something under cover of the fog. With one exception, I have kept this to myself, but before I leave here I am going to get the truth if I have to choke it out of you. And I am going to know the whereabouts of your master.

"If you want to come across with the truth now, then you will be unharmed. All that will happen will be that you will be shunted out of Egypt to-morrow before you can do any more prowling about. But if you don't come across with the truth then it won't matter when you leave Egypt, neither you nor your man, for when you do go it will be in a coffin."

"Sounds quite promising. What do you want to know?"

"Just what you were doing at the yacht in Alexandria harbour last night, and if Grant Rushton was with you."

Tony knew the moment was passed when he could keep up a tone of airy jeering. The Black Eagle meant business, and he was one of the most dangerous men at large as the young detective well knew.

Up to now he had been playing for time. The Black Eagle might risk shooting, or he might not. If he did, then he would have to take cover at once, but in view of the power of Menes, it would not be difficult for him to go into hiding, and if he and Mossop were killed why, it would be just one more mysterious pair of murders of Europeans in Cairo. It might, on the other hand, be bluff.

But the fact remained that for some reason, the Black Eagle suspected it was Tony, for one, who had been eavesdropping at the yacht, and he was out to learn the whole truth. From his last words he suspected, too, that Grant Rushton himself had been there.

And that was a suspicion that must be killed quick and hard. At any cost the fiction must be kept up for the present that Rushton was in London. So while he was still sparring for time Tony allowed himself to be seized by another racking fit of coughing.

The Black Eagle waited until the spasm was over, then:

"That isn't going to serve you one atom. For the last time—are you coming across with the truth?"

And Tony, looking into those cold eyes, knew that the moment had come when he must answer one way or the other. He could not see what Mossop was doing.

He felt the touch of the tips of the man's fingers on his shoulders, but Mossop made no attempt to convey any signal by pressure. As a matter of fact, he was standing rigid, waiting for Tony to speak, and prepared to take whichever road his words should send them.

"I guess," said Tony, looking straight into the Black Eagle's eyes, "I guess you had better shoot and be hanged then, for I shall tell you nothing."

"Then take what is coming to you!"

With that the Black Eagle jerked up the weapon and jammed his finger against the trigger. There was a crashing roar as the heavy automatic spoke, and in the same instant Tony was hurled with terrific force to one side. He struck the floor violently, and had only time to realise that he had not been struck by the bullet when the automatic spoke again, and a cry sounded behind him.

He knew now that Mossop was risking his life, had heaved him and the chair over, and in that fraction of a moment, had saved his life—for the moment at least. And at that cry he knew that Mossop had been struck by the second bullet.

Tony rolled over and came to his feet. He could see Mossop now, and the man had caught up a heavy stone funeral urn, such as are commonly found in every tomb in Egypt.

His left arm seemed to be hanging uselessly at his side, but his right was swinging back, and at the very moment he hurled it, the automatic crashed for the third time.

Tony was on his feet now, and flung round just in time to see the stone urn catch the Black Eagle full on the head.

Just beside him was a table, and from this he caught up a heavy brass electric table-lamp that had not been lighted. He janked it out of its socket, and with one jump was over the wreckage of the chair.

He rushed the Black Eagle, who was staggering about, still holding his weapon.

Tony swung the lamp with all his force, and drove it straight to its mark.

The Black Eagle lurched back against the wall, and the automatic dropped from his nerveless fingers.

Tony was on the weapon like a flash, and jammed it against the Black Eagle's temple.

"Don't you move," he panted. "If you make a shift I'll drill you clean, you murderous hound." Then he turned to Mossop, who had staggered weakly against the side of the bed.

The man's face was deathly white, and his white hand was clutching his side underneath the armpit.

"Where did he get you?" asked Tony, "in the side?"

Mossop nodded.

"Can you reach the cabinet over there? The brandy is on the bottom shelf. Try and keep up for a little while, until I dispose of this bird, Mossop, and I'll see to your wound."

"Be all right," the man mumbled, and with that he lurched along to the cabinet.

He managed to get it open, and the stopper out of the decanter; then he uptilted the receptacle, and took a deep swallow of the raw spirit. He put the decanter back and turned to Tony.

"I can manage for a bit now," he said, "what do you want me to do?"

"Do you think you can manage to scare up something with which we can gag and bind this bird? If you could pull the straps off the trunk, and get a couple of silk handkerchiefs, I could fix him."

Mossop staggered to the trunk, and by bracing one foot, succeeded in dragging out of their loops the two straps to which Tony had referred.

He dropped these on the floor beside the young detective and lurched to a chest of drawers. He opened the top one and took out several silk scarves and handkerchiefs.

All this time the Black Eagle, dazed by the blow he had received from the stone urn and the lamp, had been lying quiescent enough, but as Tony shifted his position a little he moved.

But Rushton's assistant was round on him like a flash, the barrel pressed even tighter against his temple.

"I mean it," he snarled, "one whimper out of you and you get it right through the head."

And at that the killer lay quiet again. He submitted while Tony gave the weapon to Mossop with instructions to shoot to kill if the man stirred; then he set to work with the straps, and in a few minutes had the job done securely.

Next he jammed his fingers into each side of the Black Eagle's jaw, forcing his mouth open, and before he could close it again Tony stuffed in a mixed ball of scarves and handkerchiefs, which, being silk, spread out to the full limit of the man's mouth, effectually preventing him from making any sound.

That done, Tony tied a heavy silk scarf round his mouth, and turned just in time to see Mossop topple over in a dead faint.

He sprang to his feet and got the man over on his back. He took up a knife and ripped the coat and shirt away from the arm and side.

Then he could see just where the bullet had passed, and as he saw that it had done little more than plough through between the ribs, he heaved a sigh of relief. It should not be fatal there, and the worst thing was the loss of blood.

He was an experienced hand at first-aid treatment, and he lost no time over stopping the flow of blood. He swabbed the wound dry, and then applied a pad with gauze. After that he tore away the rest of the shirt and wound a good holding bandage about Mossop's body.

He dragged him gently across to the bed and left him there while he got the decanter. Another swig of brandy when he had come round, and with Tony's aid he succeeded in getting on to the bed.

"You'll do for now," said Tony, when he saw that Mossop could understand him. "Do you think you can keep in that position?"

Mossop nodded.

"What do you want me to do?"

"I shall have to go out," said Tony. Then he bent close and spoke into the man's ear so that the Black Eagle could not hear him. "Mr. Malone must know of this without delay. I shall get into my native outfit again and find him as soon as I can. But we must not risk anyone getting this prisoner away from us. You know the Greek woman may be in on this, and she is capable of anything. If you can manage to remain conscious you could keep him and the door and window covered at the same time with the automatic."

"I give you my word of honour, sir, that I shall remain conscious. And be it man, woman or child, I shall shoot the first person who tries to enter by door or window before you return. And I'll shoot that man on the floor if he tries to get loose."

"That is just what you must do. I'll lock the door, and when I return it will be by the window. I'll have to risk leaving the cord ladder hanging from the balcony to return by. And now—Ah, steady!

Someone out in the corridor. The sound of the shots must have been heard. We shall sit tight and see what happens."

So fast had things been moving that not until that moment had it occurred to Tony that the sound of the shots must have been heard.

But the moment he heard the sound of people in the corridor, and the opening and closing of doors, he realised that, even if the adjoining rooms on either side were vacant, the sound of the automatic and the crashing of the fight must have been heard.

And Shepheard's, being a most exclusive and respectable hotel, such things could not pass without notice.

He listened while the sound of raps and voices came nearer and nearer.

Then, with a warning gesture to Mossop, he turned and made for the prostrate figure of the Black Eagle.

That individual's ears had been as sharp as Tony's, and as he saw the detective coming towards him he lifted his legs and began beating the floor with his heels as hard and as fast as possible.

Tony sprang back to the bed and grabbed a pillow.

He then lurched towards the man on the floor and, catching his legs while they were still in the air poised for another bang on the floor, he jammed the pillow beneath his heels.

He crouched, listening, and heard the sound of voices coming from, it seemed, directly across the passage.

He pushed open the door of the bathroom and caught the Black Eagle by the shoulders.

Thus he dragged him through by the same way he had entered, and just as a knock came at the corridor door of the bedroom he bent down over the killer and jerked.

"Honest, I mean this. If you give me away you may cause some trouble, but I'll get you, honest I will—before anyone can save you."

His eyes burned into those of the man on the floor.

The Black Eagle had not spent twenty years on Devil's Island— the worst of the French penal settlements—for nothing, and he knew that Tony meant business.

Grant Rushton had already said that the man known as the Black Eagle was no fool, but it was only in the future that he was to realise that, among all the criminals he had ever bucked that man was the most intelligent, if not the most cunning.

It was just then that the Black Eagle gave a sign of this, for he closed his eyes and did not look at Tony again.

Tony was taking a chance and he knew it.

But he took the chance and what he said was no bluff. He emerged from the bathroom and hurried across to Mossop. With Tony's help the man managed to get off the bed and under it.

Then, just as a knocking came at the door, Tony straightened the coverlet of the bed, and with a well-assumed paroxysm of coughing, drew his dressing gown about him and went to the door.

He unlocked it and assumed an expression of amazement as he saw several of the hotel employees standing in the corridor outside.

The spokesman was a man whom Tony recognised as the night reception clerk, a Frenchman.

"Sorry, sir," said this individual, "but complaints have been telephoned down that there has been a disturbance on this floor. Have you heard anything?"

"Disturbance? What are you talking about? The disturbance I have heard is a lot of rapping on the doors and the slamming of them. I am surprised that such a thing should be allowed at this time of night. In fact, I might have telephoned down to the office myself, only I thought it might stop."

"Then—then nothing is wrong here, sir?"

"Absolutely nothing. Would you like to come in and satisfy yourself—as long as it does not take too long and permits me to go to bed, for I am not well." Then he gave vent to another racking lit of coughing.

"No—no, sir. If everything is all right with you we shall not trouble you. And I regret that you have been disturbed."

Tony acknowledged the man's apology with a nod, and as the man bowed himself away, closed the door. He stood a while until he heard them proceeding down the corridor to the door of the next room, then he tiptoed across to the bed and helped Mossop to get back on the mattress.

As soon as that was accomplished he re-entered the bathroom and had a look at the Black Eagle.

That individual was lying just as he had left him, and Tony felt a little thrill as he realised that he had "backed down" a man such as he.

He dragged him back into the bedroom, where Mossop could keep him covered with the pistol; then he lost no time in getting ready to make a journey through the night to Cairo to find Lawrence

Malone. For he knew that, in Rushton's absence, the Secret Service man must be told what had taken place.

* * * * *

Lawrence Malone was seated in the den of his very modest quarters, clad in pyjamas and dressing-gown and enjoying a final nightcap, when his most trusted man entered to inform him that there was a native outside who insisted on seeing him.

Malone had had a stirring time of it during the past few days, and he was a little irritated at being disturbed at that hour of the night. Therefore, he sent the man back to ask if the message could not be delivered in the morning.

But when the man came back and repeated a single word which he had been told to say, Malone jerked his head up sharply.

"Yes, yes; show him in at once!" he ordered.

A few minutes later the native was brought in, and Malone needed only one glance to know that it was Tony. He dismissed the man—though he was quite as trustworthy, in his way, as Mossop—and as soon as the door closed came to his feet.

"What is it, Tony?" he asked quickly. "Come here and sit down. What has happened since I left you near the hotel?"

Tony dropped into a seat and related briefly what had occurred.

"Mossop is badly hurt, though not dangerously wounded, Mr. Malone. I have the Black Eagle safe, and I think Mossop will be able to keep him so. But after the inquiries that were made it is too risky to leave him there. Something must be done, but the dickens of it is I have a hunch the Greek woman suspects the same thing about the guv'nor and me that he suspected. I thought the best thing was to put it up to you."

"Quite right, Tony, and fine work—fine work. Devil of a good job bagging the Black Eagle like that. From what Rushton has told me he is a real man-eater, and yet you and Mossop bagged him."

"It was Mossop, Mr. Malone. If it hadn't been for Mossop I should have been as dead as the Sphinx by now. But what do you advise, sir?"

"Give me a few moments. Let me think." With that Malone began pacing up and down the floor, while Tony sat brooding. At last the big man came to a stop, and with a gesture that was habitual with him, wagged his finger at Tony.

"This is going to bring some phases of this affair to a crisis, Tony.

I should have liked it better—and I am sure Rushton would have agreed with me—if this had not happened; or if it had to happen, if it had taken place a week or ten days hence. But what is done is done, and thank heaven you and Mossop managed to get the upper hand. I agree with you that the Black Eagle must have figured things out for himself, even while he was on board the yacht at Alexandria. A dangerous man, that. And a clever one, too, for he was cunning enough to keep it to himself."

"He mentioned something about another person, sir."

"Um, yes, well, that must mean the Greek woman. It can't be Menes. From what Rushton said to me I gather that he is still a little puzzled as to just why the Black Eagle has mixed up in this business. It is a queer mixture altogether, and Rushton thinks that, if it is meant to be a permanent confederation among them, there will be a good deal of internal politics going on before they finish. He also said that in that weakness would lie our strength. So I think that we may take it that if he did confide in anyone, it was the Greek woman. If so, then she must know of the visit of the Black Eagle to you this evening. In that case, while she may be safe enough for to-night, she will begin to wonder about things if she doesn't see him in the morning. Which means that both of them must be swept out of the way."

"What about Prince Menes, Mr. Malone?"

"That is just the big problem, Tony. I take it that Madame Goupolis must report to him at stated intervals and, if she doesn't, then he is bound to make enquiries. Rushton told me about that Monte Carlo affair, and, from what I know personally of Menes, I am sure that he will again become suspicious of her if she drops out of sight. It is the very devil of a puzzle, but it must be solved—and quickly."

"What about snaffling Menes as well?" asked Tony after a pause.

Malone stopped abruptly and smiled at Tony.

"You have Rushton's daring all right, Tony, but that would be too risky. If Menes should disappear the White Flag gang would at once turn out in full force to find him. No. We must think of something else."

Again he paced up and down the room, and it seemed to Tony that he meant to go on all night, when he came to an abrupt halt.

"There is one way that I can see, and just one way, Tony. This is it."

Then he began to speak, and as Tony listened he realised that

Malone had, indeed, hit on a solution, if—and a very big if—it could be brought off.

It was quite as daring a plan as he, Tony, had suggested, but it had the additional merit that it held a chance of pulling the wool over Menes' eyes for the time being, and that meant everything to Rushton's plans.

Half an hour later, Lawrence Malone, back in his native dress and concealed by a voluminous burnous, was taking a way by the back streets of Cairo towards Shepheard's Hotel. And trotting along by his side was the same "Arab" who had stolen out of the place an hour or so before.

CHAPTER 15.

They re-entered the hotel the way Tony had left it.

As far as the latter could see, things were unchanged. Mossop still lay on the bed, with the automatic trained on the Black Eagle; the latter was as securely bound and gagged as ever, and the wicker-chair lay just as it had been overturned.

Mossop looked pretty white but was still game, for he smiled as he saw Tony, and, in answer to his quick enquiry, protested that he was all right. Malone, who had had a very wide experience in the treatment of wounds (he had, as a matter of fact, taken his medical degree at Dublin, but had never practised) made an examination, and pronounced Tony's first-aid treatment as all that could have been desired.

"But you must be got away from here and receive regular attention," he added. But he did not explain to Mossop just why it was that he must not remain at the hotel.

Then Malone stood over the Black Eagle, studying him. The Black Eagle knew now, of course, that the big man in the white garments and the burnous must be a European in disguise; but he had never seen him before, and did not know just where to place him. All he was sure of was that it was not Grant Rushton.

Finally, Malone motioned for Tony to follow him into the bathroom. When they went out of earshot of their prisoner, he said in a low tone:

"He is a new one to me, but he looks like a man who could be dangerous."

"And he can—I can vouch for that!" responded Tony.

"Do you know where his room is?"

"Yes."

"And that of the Greek woman?"

"Yes—if she is occupying the same one which she had before going to Alexandria."

"Have you gone through the prisoner's clothes?"

"No, sir; I was too anxious to get to you to tell you what had happened."

"Well, I think we shall see if we can find anything. I have a plan—if we can work it."

They returned to the bedroom then, and with practised fingers Malone went through the pockets of the Black Eagle's coat and trousers. He found money in both notes and gold; a gold pencil and a gold-edged tablet, on two or three pages of which the owner had scribbled memoranda about appointments and bets.

There was a cigarette-case and a few letters addressed to "David Stone"—the name under which the Black Eagle was known at the hotel. A few other trinkets of no importance, and that was all.

Malone laid everything but the gold-edged tablet on one side, and, with this in his hand, seated himself at the small writing-table.

He drew a piece of paper towards him and, picking up Tony's fountain-pen, began to copy some of the words which were written on the tablet.

He experimented for some minutes while Tony watched him; then he tore off the pages of the tablet which bore writing, and began to scribble something on a clean sheet. Tony, watching, saw that this was what he wrote:

"Come, if possible, at once. Most important."

He neither signed it nor initialled it. He tore off the page and folded it once. Then he slipped it in one of the hotel envelopes and turned to Tony.

"What is the number of the Greek woman's room?" he asked in a whisper which could not reach the Black Eagle.

"It was a hundred and nineteen, but I'll ask Mossop if she has changed. He will know."

Tony crossed to the bed and whispered the question to Mossop. The man confirmed the number which Tony had given, adding that she had not changed her room. Tony nodded to Malone, who slipped the folded paper in the envelope and sealed it. Then he wrote just the number, "119," on the outside, and rose. He stood midway between the bed and where the Black Eagle lay, and, turning to the killer, said:

"This man had his orders, and they are not going to be changed. If you try any tricks he is going to shoot—and shoot to kill." Then, to Mossop: "You understand, Mossop?"

"Yes, sir, and I'll do it."

"Don't hesitate; I take full responsibility."

Then he signed to Tony and motioned him to open the door leading into the corridor.

Tony unlocked it and they stepped out. He closed the door after him and they stood listening. Not a sound could they hear, for it was now very late, and they both knew the hotel well enough to figure that they were not likely to meet any servants about then. If they did, all they could do would be to handle the situation when it arose.

"His room first," whispered Malone, showing a room-key which he had taken from among the contents of the Black Eagle's pockets.

Tony started on and, after traversing first one corridor and then another, stopped before a door.

"Eighty-seven," he said, in a whisper, "this is it."

Malone inserted the key and turned it.

The door opened at once, and they stepped inside. There was a light burning, and one glance was sufficient to show them that it was a man's room, and at that moment the occupant was out. Malone closed the door and took the envelope from beneath his burnous.

"This is my plan, Tony," he said. "We have got to get that man out of the hotel to-night. And we have got to take the woman away as well. I know where I can keep them safely for as long as is necessary—or, at any rate, until I can consult with Rushton. We dare not drag her from her room, but if we can decoy her here, we can turn the trick. This is just a hasty shot at imitating the Black Eagle's handwriting, but it may pass. She may not suspect a trick. If she really knows on what errand he was going to-night she will be anxious to know the result. That is what I am counting on. Do you think you can slip through to a hundred and nineteen and push this under her door."

"Sure, sir. It isn't far from here. When I slip it under, shall I knock?"

"If you can get away before she opens the door and sees you."

"I'll manage that, all right."

So, taking the note, Tony opened the door and disappeared.

Malone stood just within, waiting, and it was only a few minutes later that a light tap came from outside.

He opened the door quickly and Tony slipped into the room.

"All serene, sir. There was a light in her room —I could see it over the door. I pushed the note under, and gave it a tap and then disappeared. I was round the bend into the corridor before she could possibly get the door open to look out."

"Good, all we can do now is to wait. Stand here close to the handle of the door. I shall stand behind it. If she comes, open the door and, if possible, let her get inside before she sees you. Then we will both tackle her. You pay more attention to the door. I shall go for her mouth and throat. She must not be allowed to scream, and remember,

Tony, that in this case her sex doesn't matter two pins. She is as dangerous as a cobra."

They took up their positions and stood waiting.

Perhaps five minutes went by when there came a light tap at the door.

Tony turned the handle and swung it open.

A cloaked figure stepped in like a shadow, and Tony closed the door just as Malone threw himself forward. Before the startled woman knew what was happening he had one hand over her mouth and another at her throat, while Tony, forgetting her sex for the moment, grabbed her arms.

She struggled and kicked, and would have bitten Malone's hand if she could have got her teeth into it. But they were not taking any chances, and in about two minutes Malone's far from gentle methods had her as quiet as a lamb.

He motioned then for Tony to open the door, and, holding the woman in a vice-like grip, he pushed her into the corridor.

Tony followed, closing the door, and between them they rushed her as silently as possible back along the corridors to Tony's room. Tony opened the door, and Malone forced her inside.

Her eyes had been burning with a terrible rage at the way she had been handled, but as she saw the Black Eagle lying trussed up on the floor they clouded in deepest puzzlement. For the first time she began to realise the sort of trap she had fallen into.

But Malone and Tony gave her no time to renew her struggles. Tony dragged out some cords and more scarves and handkerchiefs, and, while Malone held her, the lad tied her wrists and gagged her, attending to the latter first.

He didn't accomplish it without getting a savage bite from her sharp white teeth, but after that effort Malone held her jaw in such a way that she couldn't repeat it.

If they both could have been annihilated by her eyes they would have shrivelled to dust on the spot, for never were woman's eyes more murderous than those of the Goupolis in that moment.

Next, Tony secured her ankles, and after setting up the wicker-chair, they forced her into it. Still they used more cords, binding her into the chair, and Tony finished up the job by putting a couple of cushions under her feet, so she could not make a row if she took it into her head to start drumming on the floor with her heels.

Then they desisted, and, as their eyes met, a look of mutual congratulation passed between them. But the job was only started, as they knew, and Tony waited eagerly for what Malone had to say next. The explorer walked across to Mossop.

"If we help you down the ladder do you think you could manage to come with me?" he asked.

Mossop nodded at once.

"Yes, sir, I can manage all right. If I could have another swig of spirit I could keep on going the rest of the night."

"That won't be necessary, but you shall have the brandy just the same."

Tony poured out a generous allowance, and when Mossop had drunk it they assisted him to the window.

"We'll get him down and I'll handle him after that. You can look for me to return inside half an hour, Tony. I'll bring a car this time and two or three of my most trusted men. Then we'll lose no time in getting our birds away. In the meantime you will have to watch them."

"I'll watch them all right," responded the lad grimly. "They will be safe enough until you get back."

Then they got Mossop down the ladder, and Tony stood for a few moments while the pair lurched off through the garden to the lane at the back. As soon as they had vanished he returned to the bedroom and took out the automatic. He turned to Madame Goupolis and eyed her. Then:

"You have seen enough by now to know that we mean business. And you can take it from me, Madame, that your sex is not going to help you if you try any tricks. You know why without being told."

With that he sat down on the side of the bed and held the pistol so that he could keep them both covered.

The Black Eagle had turned over on his side, so that he could look at the woman, and, as he saw the man was trying to flash some message with his eyes, Tony got up again and dragged the wicker-chair round so her back was towards the man.

Then he grinned at the Black Eagle.

"Better give it up," he said. "When I say I mean business I mean that and nothing else. You tried your best to kill me to-night, and you very nearly did so but for my companion. And for that reason alone I wouldn't at all mind finding some reason to plug you. So you had better take your medicine when you have to."

And the Black Eagle, dangerous as he was, could do nothing but glare unutterable threats, which didn't worry Tony in the least.

At that point the Greek woman began drumming her heels and managed to kick the cushion aside. Tony was over in a flash, and, catching the chair by the front, tilted it well back until it threatened to go over completely.

"I'll keep you with your heels in the air," he snapped, "unless you stop that game. Are you going to do as I say?"

She nodded, her eyes furious, and Tony set her down again.

Then he took up his place on the side of the bed, and he was still there when there came a slight sound from the direction of the veranda.

He swung sharply, the automatic ready for instant use, but he gave a sigh of slight relief as he saw Lawrence Malone come in through the window, followed by three other figures dressed like himself.

They went at the rest of the job without a moment's delay, taking the woman first.

They lowered her down the cord ladder and carried her through the garden.

They were back in a few moments to take the Black Eagle, and as the second prisoner disappeared Tony turned to Malone.

"Where are you taking them?"

"To my own house, Tony. I have taken Mossop there too. I shall have one of our own doctors look after him. It just happens that my place has a zenana annexe[1]. It used to belong to a wealthy Egyptian, and I shall keep the woman and the Black Eagle there until I have had a word with Rushton. I am going to force the woman to write a note to Prince Menes, which will tell him that she has been forced to leave Cairo for a few days on an important matter connected with her business for the White Flag Society."

"What if she refuses?"

"She won't refuse. I have a woman there who will see that she does what she is told, or —."

And he grunted expressively.

"What about you, Tony?"

---

[1] *A part of a house belonging to a Hindu or Muslim family and reserved for the women of the household.*

112

"I think I shall remain here until we hear from the guv'nor. Those were his orders."

"All right. But you can come to my place if you wish. It is almost morning, and as soon as things get going I shall have a hint dropped from the right quarter that no further enquiries are to be made about the sound of shooting that was heard to-night."

"Very good, sir."

With that Malone took himself off, and, after drawing up the cord ladder and putting it away in one of his boxes, Tony set to work to get rid of his disguise. He was ready enough for bed when that was finished, for he had had no real sleep for nearly forty-eight hours.

He was almost asleep as soon as his head hit the pillow, and the next thing he realised was the room telephone ringing insistently.

He stumbled out of bed and across to the table. He took off the receiver and said "Hallo." A voice answered him—a cautious voice—which he recognised as Malone's.

"I have had a message," it said. "Meet me at the same place to-night not later than eight. Do you understand?"

"Yes." And before he could say more he heard a click at the other end.

Tony turned and stood frowning.

"A message from the guv'nor," he muttered. "It can't be possible. Why, he can't have done much more than reach the place at this hour of the morning."

Then he walked to the dressing-table and looked at his watch which lay there. And as he saw the hour he gave a low whistle.

"My sainted aunt!" he ejaculated. "Half-past four in the afternoon, and I thought it was midmorning at latest. I must have slept like a log for ten solid hours!"

* * * * *

Tony stuck to his room until evening. He did not want to run into Jack or his sister, and when he ordered dinner to be brought up he cautioned the white-clad servant not to mention that he was back. He accompanied this with a terrible fit of coughing, and the man took it for granted that he was too ill to be seen.

Of course, Tony did not expect really to be disturbed, for he knew that Malone could pull powerful strings, and he took it for granted that he had done so early in the morning, as he had said he would.

At seven o'clock he packed a small bag, and after a close scrutiny of the gardens, dropped it down among some bushes. He knew of the existence of a back staircase that gave on to the garden, so he made his way cautiously by this route to the door he was seeking.

He had not got into his Arab disguise, for he did not know just what was afoot, and he was going to take a chance on reaching the Thieves' Hut without being spotted. He retrieved his small bag all right, and then swiftly made his way into the lane.

He walked along until he reached a broader street, and there got a taxi. He gave the man instructions to drive out to the Meni House Road, and when he knew they were some three furlongs from the spot where he would leave the road to reach the hut he had the man pull up.

He paid him generously, and, because he was used to the crazy ways of tourists, the man thought little of the fact that his fare chose to proceed on foot. He turned the taxi and drove back towards Cairo, while Tony kept in the shade of the trees on the left-hand side so as not to be spotted by anyone in the string of cars that were still coming back from Gizeh.

He watched his chance to leave the road, and once away from it made a cautious but quick journey to the hut. He swung in through the window, and then, as his feet touched the floor, he was greeted by a blinding flash of a torch full in his eyes. It went out next instant, and as he stumbled forward he heard Malone's voice.

"You didn't get into your other things; well, I couldn't tell you over the 'phone to do so, but I can see you have a bag, so I suppose you brought them?"

"Yes, sir, you didn't say and I didn't know what was up. It won't take me ten minutes, and I don't need a light."

"Then make haste, for we ride as soon as possible."

As Tony stripped he asked about Rushton.

"All I know is from what I made of a short code letter which reached me this afternoon. He is at the oasis and wants us to come out this evening. I judge he must have run his quarry to earth— stout fellow, that master of yours. I suppose he told you that one part of the job for me to attend to was to cable to England for two civil planes to come out here on the double quick?"

"Yes, he did, Mr. Malone."

"Well, I have had a reply. They are already on their way, and are in charge of the men Rushton wanted me to try to get to come."

"You mean Alan Rayne, I suppose," mumbled Tony, as he finished smearing his face and neck, and began to get into his Arab clothes.

"Quite right. If things go as we plan there should be quite an interesting little reception waiting for that yacht when she gets back. Now are you ready? Then come on. The horses are waiting not far away."

Tony followed him through the window, and together they went along in the direction of the Meni House Road.

They took a parallel course by this for about a quarter of a mile, and then, suddenly in a small grove of trees, they came upon three horses in charge of a white burnoused figure.

He rose at once as they came up, and without a word passed one bridle rein to Malone and another to Tony.

Then all three swung into the saddle, and a few seconds later, like wraithes of night, they were flying across the desert, the waning moon low in the east beside them, and the three colossal Pyramids to their left.

Thirty-six miles it was to the oasis of El Adid, and they covered it without a halt.

Their Arab horses shook off the sandy miles without the slightest sign of fatigue, and it was only when the third man, whom Tony did not know, uttered a word to Malone that they slackened pace.

They then proceeded at a trot until they came to a small grove of date palms on the outskirts of the oasis, where they dismounted.

A white-garbed figure suddenly loomed up in front of them, and Tony heard their guide carry on a low-toned conversation with him.

Then he turned to Malone and spoke in Arabic. Following that Malone touched Tony's arm.

"Everything is all right," he said, in a low tone, "Rushton is waiting. We are to follow this fellow."

They started off at once, keeping away from the few scattered houses which lay in the oasis. There might have been a hundred persons living there, or none, so far as Tony could judge, for it was as silent as the grave.

But he knew the country well enough to realise that scores of pairs of eyes might be following them and their every movement.

Then suddenly their guide swung to the left, and a few paces farther on a low hut loomed up directly in front of them. He made for this and, just before reaching the open door, gave vent to an odd sound.

At once a reply came from the interior of the hut, and at a sign from the guide they went on. He disappeared inside, and a second later Tony felt a quick thrill as he heard Rushton's tone bidding them come in. He peered through the black opening and thought he saw what looked like the glow of a cigarette.

He could smell smoke, too. Then Malone got his flash lamp switched on and, standing on the threshold, the pair saw Rushton in his beggar's robes, seated on the ground, smoking as imperturbably as if he were back in the consulting-room at Jermyn Street.

Lying bound and gagged on the mud floor beside him was a bulky white bundle, which they found a few seconds later was none other than Flash Brady, or, as he preferred to be known at that time, Sakr-el-Droog, the Hawk of the Peak.

A closer examination revealed that Rushton was decidedly the worse for wear. Before leaving the Thieves' Hut his clothes had appeared to be the last word in rags; but now they were nothing but strips of torn cloth, and when they looked at the wreckage of the savage countenance of Brady, whose cheeks were cut and caked with dried blood, and whose forked beard was tangled and matted with blood, they knew that a battle royal must have taken place between these two before Grant Rushton calmly sat himself down to send his message to Malone.

But it was not until after, that Rushton told the full story of his fight. All he vouchsafed on this occasion was:

"Glad you got here all right—you see I found our bird in the nest. Bit of a dispute, but I finally got him to listen to reason. Bit of a problem how to get a note to you, and our friend here bid pretty high to get the folks to release him and kick me into the desert—always knew this type would sell itself to the highest bidder, and it happened that I was more plentifully supplied with actual funds than our friend—cash counts after all, with the result that it looks as if we may get away without further trouble. Suppose you have fixed things at your end, Malone?"

"You bet I—or should I say we have; for things happened in Cairo last night, and thanks to Tony, we snaffled another pair of birds. It had to be done—they were suspicious of that business at the yacht."

Then Malone told Rushton all that had taken place, and when he had finished, Rushton nodded approval.

"That was the only thing to do. Did you persuade the Goupolis to write the letter to Menes?"

"She wrote it all right—and at dictation," answered Malone grimly, but he didn't explain how it was done.

They discussed ways and means for some time longer, with the result that it was decided to take Brady back to Cairo, and keep him incarcerated with the rest.

Malone explained that he had had a report just before leaving that Wu Ling had come out of hiding, and had taken up his quarters at the Savoy in full style, and had produced official documents showing that he was visiting Egypt on official business for the Chinese Government, in order to study their methods of cotton production.

That put him out of their reach for the time being, but it also kept him in the open which, Rushton and Malone figured, was just about the same thing.

The man who had guided them to the hut produced two more horses, and, when he had been rewarded, they got the raging Brady into the saddle and saw that he was well tied there.

Then Rushton took the bridle rein as a lead, and the little cavalcade set off on the return to Cairo.

It was just five o'clock in the morning when they again reached the Thieves' Hut. Here they slid to the ground, sore and stiff, but content with things so far.

The man who had accompanied them disappeared with the horses, while Rushton, Malone and Tony, with Brady in their midst, walked towards the Meni House Road.

A Secret Service car was waiting for them there, and they got in at once.

They drove straight to Malone's house, where they entered unobserved, and, after seeing Brady safely locked away, Malone showed Rushton and Tony the rooms they would occupy until it was time to make the next move.

The sun was just rimming the east when they finally bade each other good-night, but even then Tony would not turn in until Rushton had told him about the fight with Brady at El Adid.

And in his turn Tony had to give details of just how they had bested the Black Eagle and kidnapped Madame Goupolis.

In the former victory Rushton seemed to see a most important gain, and those were his last words to his assistant as he started for his room.

CHAPTER 16.

During the next two days Malone sent every Secret Service man he could mobilise to Alexandria and that part of the coast.

They had explicit instructions what to watch for, and to report by telegraph in triplicate and code the moment they had anything.

Four days later Alan Rayne, accompanied by another machine, arrived at the aerodrome at Heliopolis, and Rushton sent a message to Rayne, telling him to stand by for urgent flight if necessary.

In the meantime, Malone contrived to get both machines loaded with six bombs each, and from that they had nothing to do but to sit tight and wait for something to happen.

It did.

On the eighth morning after their return from the oasis of El Adid a code message reached Malone, which sent them into action.

Early that afternoon they motored out to Heliopolis—Rushton, Malone and Tony, and one of Malone's lieutenants.

They found Rayne and his men on the job, and within twenty minutes of their arrival were off, ostensibly on a purely civil flight to Haifa, in Palestine.

It was early morning when they reached the coast to the west of Alexandria, and there they flew low so that Malone could pick up certain signals which were being wagged from a concealed wadi (valley).

Rushton read them, too, and signed to Alan Rayne to fly out to sea and in a westernly direction.

He and Tony were with Rayne, while Malone and his man were in another machine.

The latter followed Rayne's course, but it was almost dusk before Rushton lifted his arm and pointed to something on the sea a thousand feet beneath them.

Tony saw it too, and it needed just one look to tell him that it was the yacht "Sultan."

Rayne and the other avaitor had their instructions, and, as they spotted the yacht, both machines dropped from the thousand-foot level in a long slide until they were less than three hundred feet above the water.

About two miles away was the sandy, barren coast to the west of Alexandria, and as he looked back Rushton saw that the heavy sea mist was already beginning to sweep in from the sea. There would be no moon until the early hours of the following morning, and he shifted in his seat as he realised that what they had to do must be done quickly, or even then their quarry might escape.

Still, after long argument, they had agreed to give those on board the yacht a chance to get away.

The whole shore was dotted with Secret Service men, and if they made that way, there was little chance for them to escape.

As for Mathew Cardolak and the Three Musketeers, Rushton didn't care two straws what happened to them, but he reasoned there might be some innocent persons among the crew and, if so, they deserved a chance to save their lives.

For this reason, on their first swoop over the yacht the two 'planes dropped a bomb each in the water, that from Rayne's machine falling a hundred yards or so ahead, and the other about the same distance astern.

It was a warning which would be understood easily enough by those on the yacht if, as Rushton thought, they were guilty, and as the 'planes came about, they saw that it had, indeed, been read and understood.

They could see a frantic running about on the decks, and boat after boat was dropped into the water. Men poured into them, but they could not see if Cardolak and the Three Musketeers were among them.

They circled again, and watched the boats pull madly away; circled out to sea, and then returned, watching the yacht begin to change her course in an erratic manner.

Then Rushton lifted his hand high, and at the signal Rayne and the other pilot swooped up to a higher level, and came back directly over the yacht.

Almost at the same instant a bomb hurtled downward from each, and each was a perfect hit. The result was appalling. There was the almost simultaneous explosion of the two bombs as they struck, then the whole yacht seemed to be torn asunder as the decks opened up and the terrible cargo of mines which she was carrying blew her to atoms.

One moment she was, the next she was not. One moment she had been a graceful creature of the sea, the next she was nothing but a few scattered bits of wreckage, floating on the water.

If they had needed any proof of the nature of the cargo she carried and the dastardly purpose for which it was intended, they had it in full measure and overflowing in that annihilating explosion.

And the boats—what of them?

So interested had those in the two 'planes been to watch the result of the bombing that they had forgotten to follow the course of the fleeing boats. And now, as they gazed downwards, they saw nothing but the blank face of a wide stretch of mist over the water.

Somewhere beneath that blanket were the boats, if they had escaped the effects of the terrible concussion which followed on the blowing up of the yacht.

Rayne looked at Rushton as if to ask if he would unload his bombs on the chance of bagging some of them, and Malone signalled the same query.

But Rushton gave a negative in each case.

Night had now fallen.

They could only make for the shore, and if they landed there the Secret Service men should be able to snaffle them.

So both machines unloaded their bombs over blank water at the edge of the mist, and as the sound of the last one died away, they turned and sped back towards Heliopolis.

Some of the fugitives from the yacht did reach the shore and, as Rushton had figured, were immediately snaffled by the Secret Service men there.

But not a sign was there of Mathew Cardolak or the Three Musketeers, and as the days passed without news of them, Rushton began to think that the concussion had sent them under.

If they, and they alone, had gone down, he would have been devoutly thankful. To be hoist by their own petard would have been a fitting end to such a terrible crime, which they had attempted to carry out.

The survivors were brought into Cairo for examination, for by then Rushton and Malone were able to advance such an undoubted case that even the Egyptian authorities were able to move at last.

At the right moment Malone produced the Black Eagle, Madame Goupolis, and Brady. A searching enquiry was supposed to be started, but after hanging about Cairo for the better part of a week without receiving any summons to appear as a witness, he gave it up in disgust, and prepared to return to London.

"Just as I thought," he stormed. "It isn't the Government itself, but the treachery with which its offices are all honeycombed."

He heard indirectly that Menes had been called up for a questioning, but had denied all knowledge of any such plot, and, of course, he was not held.

It would take a courageous Government in that country to hold Prince Menes.

Wu Ling continued on his bland way at his hotel, and, in view of the official diplomatic papers which he held, nothing could be done.

The Goupolis made a silent escape from prison one night, and in that it was easy to see the hand of Menes.

Then, on the very next night, both the Black Eagle and Brady escaped, and with that Rushton clamped the lid on his boxes.

"Enough for me," he snapped, at Tony's query as to what he was going to do. "We leave for London to-morrow. The only consolation is that Mathew Cardolak and the Three Musketeers seem to have gone to perdition with the yacht."

"Well, that's something anyway," answered Tony. "And Mr. Malone says that the really great thing is that you discovered the plot, and frustrated it in time to save the Suez Canal and the ships which would be passing through after the mines were laid."

"Enough. Enough. Do you call that enough when we had the whole gang bagged and under lock and key, the whole caboodle, with the exception of Wu Ling and Menes?" Then Rushton's voice grew calmer. "That isn't all, Tony," he said. "What is worrying me is that this is the first blow they have planned. In my opinion, we have seen the beginning of one of the biggest, most powerful, and most deadly criminal combinations ever formed, and I miss my guess very badly if we don't see signs of their work again in the very near future."

And Grant Rushton was right, as events proved.

CHAPTER 17.

Their luggage was actually being taken down by the porters, and Rushton and Tony were in the lounge when a note was handed to Rushton.

He moved aside and opened the envelope. The note was signed with Malone's initials.

"Please hold everything, Rushton. Most important and urgent developments. Must see you earliest possible moment. Will come round to hotel the moment I finish off some stuff here."

Rushton sighed. He was fed up with everything in Cairo and in the whole of Egypt. But he had little difficulty in guessing that something had developed afresh in connection with the canal affair.

"Stop the porters, Tony," he ordered. "We are not going, after all. I'll have a word at the reception desk."

Such a sudden change in plans was all in the day's work to Tony. As a matter of fact, he wasn't at all unwilling to remain if it meant a further brush with Menes and the others. He knew Rushton was by no means content with what had seemed the finale of the affair, and curiously, what galled him personally more than anything else was the apparent escape of the Three Musketeers, for he did not believe that they had been killed in the destruction of the ship. The explanation of this lies probably in the fact that those three were nearer to Tony's own age than any of the others.

He passed the word to the porters and waited by the lift until Rushton joined him. Rushton was smiling grimly.

"I have usually found hotel servants too hard-boiled to reveal surprise over anything," he murmured, "but I shook that slick young man at the reception desk out of his stride."

Tony grinned and glanced across to where the clerk was still shaking his head in astonishment.

"He must think we like the hotel so well we can't leave."

"Exactly what I told him, Tony."

Back in their rooms, however, they became serious enough.

"What do you suppose it is?" Tony pressed Rushton.

"I should say our friends have not taken their beating. We know that Menes isn't going to see everything go smash if he can help it. It must have cost him a pretty penny, one way and another, to bring things up to such a point. Then he has Wu Ling still to reckon with. From what we know of that yellow devil, we can be sure he isn't going back to China without something more than a sick headache. I'll wager he drove a hard bargain with Menes."

"What do you think about Mathew Cardolak and the Three Musketeers, chief?"

"I wish I knew, Tony. On the face of it, one is tempted to gamble that they were wiped out, but— I don't know. It is extraordinary how many lives some of these crooks seem to possess. If Cardolak did survive, then we can count him in with Menes. He is a rich man, one of the richest in the world I should say. A few thousands here and there is no more than chicken-feed to him. And against that is his genuine passion for Egyptology."

"Well, guv', if the Black Eagle and Brady pop up again, it looks like being a nice little party."

"We shall know something when Malone comes, and, by the same token, I wish he would hurry. Something definite and urgent must have reached him to bring a note like he sent."

It was half an hour before Malone did turn up, but he brought plenty of news with him.

"I'm uncommonly glad that I caught you in time, Rushton. There's the devil to pay."

"In the form of Menes, I suppose?"

"You've said it. Menes is on the rampage."

"What has he broken?"

"I should say about a dozen different things. Wu Ling has vanished. Menes is at his palace, with armed guards of his own outside the gates. There's a nerve for you, and the Government isn't doing a thing about it."

"Menes must think his position unassailable."

"He does, it is open defiance. And, of course, it means one thing."

"That he is going all out for a final effort."

"Exactly. It means, too, that he has connected all the loose ends again. And that isn't the whole of it. Brady and the Black Eagle are free. They are now at Menes' palace. We might as well have shut them up in a paper gaol. The Goupolis is there, too, and I've just had an underground tip that your friends, Mathew Cardolak and the Three Musketeers escaped after all."

"Talk about the gathering of the clans," muttered Tony.

"You've said a mouthful, Tony."

Malone looked terribly worried as he paced the floor.

"And that isn't the half of it," he went on. "There is a lot of new trouble in several cases."

"That looks like Sakr-el-Droog," put in Rushton.

"Brady, I think you're right, Rushton. But what seems to me to be the worst feature of all is a very grave rumour that reached me just before I left the office to come here. I have it from one of my agents in Alexandria, a fellow I trust thoroughly that a strange submarine has been snooping about off the Egyptian coast. It hasn't been identified as belonging to any known fleet with a Mediterranean patrol. It is known to have been near the spot where you bombed Cardolak's yacht. I've been wondering whether it is connected with him."

"There is every possibility. I wish I had known about this before. I should have remained in Alexandria. But what do you expect me to do? What can I do now? It seems useless to round up any of Menes' gang. Unless you can tighten up things in another direction, it is a hopeless job."

Malone moved closer.

"I've done that. A long secret report was sent to London. Someone very high up is taking a personal interest in this job now. In fact, you will find that Menes will not be able to slip the nooses of those birds if you can corral them again. The reason I sent the note round to you was because you were mentioned personally. We have been instructed to use every method to keep you here. And at the same time I must warn you of the very grave danger from assassination. Menes will get you before you are out of Cairo if he can."

Scarcely had he uttered the last word before a bullet crashed through the Venetian blinds, and ripped past Rushton so close as to rip the sleeve of the silk jacket he was wearing.

It was embedded in the wall, and the sound of the gun from which it had been discharged had died away by the time Rushton and Malone recovered from the monetary paralysis that held them, Tony was already plunging towards the window.

"Look out!"

It was Rushton who shouted the warning, and well was it he did so, for, on the same instant, there came a stream of lead through the blind, accompanied by a string of explosions that was almost as rapid as those of a machine-gun.

Lying flat on the floor, they waited until the racketing finished. Even through the blinds the strong smell of cordite reached them. But, daring though the attack was, the would-be assassins were taking a dreadful risk. Because of that or because they believed their purpose accomplished, they fled from the veranda where the ambush had been staged.

Tony smashed through the Venetian blind, his gun jerking up as he went. Rushton and Malone were close behind him. Far down the veranda they saw two natives running at top speed.

Rushton and Malone also had their guns out now, and, just before the two figures dived down the stairs that led to the gardens, all three weapons were going.

One bullet must have found a mark, for they saw one of the flying men vanish headfirst from view. Yet when they reached the top of the stairs he was nowhere to be seen. But bloodstains made a trail, step by step, to the bottom of the flight, and at the landing there was a small pool where the wounded man had paused.

There were none beyond, however, not a trace to show where he had gone from there, although there was still another flight to negotiate before reaching the garden.

Rushton looked over the veranda railing. Tony was already racing down the second flight of stairs. Malone was casting about uncertainly, then he gave vent to an oath.

"They've gone into one of the rooms along here, Rushton. Look out, they may shoot from cover."

Rushton let Tony carry on. It was still possible that the assassins had reached the garden, though, in that case, it certainly looked as though one must be carrying the other.

He and Malone were moving along the veranda when a loud scream burst in a nearby room. It was the scream of a woman, laden with terror.

Malone leaped to some closed Venetian blinds and tore them aside. In the room a woman screamed again. Malone, preparing to use the authority of his position, leapt into the room with Rushton at his heels.

They saw a young woman cowering against the wall, her eyes frightened, her hands clutching a flimsy dressing-gown. Rushton recognised her as one of a party of American tourists he had seen about the hotel.

The door of the room was open, and, seeing Rushton and Malone had something less threatening than what had just passed through, she pointed to the door.

"Th-that way!" she chattered.

Rushton threw her a quick word of reassurance.

"It's all right, they won't harm you now."

Then he and Malone were through the door, racing along the corridor while the girl still wondered what dreadful business was afoot. There was some excuse for her terror, for, on emerging from her bath-room, she had seen a terrifying native smash through into the room, a gun in one hand and a prone form over his shoulder.

Rushton and Malone reached the end of the corridor where it broadened to a wide landing by the lift well. Not a sign of their quarry did they see. If they had gone by the stairs there was just a chance of intercepting them in the lounge, for, even though they had already taken such chances, it did not seem likely they would have the nerve to pass through the lounge of that de luxe hotel in such a state.

With the influence of Prince Menes behind them, however, both Rushton and Malone knew that they would stop at little.

The stopping of the lift turned their attention in that direction.

The gate rolled back and the gate-man looked at them enquiringly. Malone questioned him rapidly, eliciting absolutely nothing of value.

The man had seen no one such as Malone described. He had come up to this floor because the bell had rung from that number. He thought Malone and Rushton must have summoned him.

They exchanged glances and then Malone drew Rushton's attention to the well of the luggage lift that adjoined the passenger elevators. Through the glass panels of the door they could see the wire cable moving.

"That's how they went, old man. They jabbed the button of the passenger lift so as to keep the lift-man busy, and went down in the luggage lift. They're away by a back entrance now unless Tony has intercepted them."

"There's a small chance of that," returned Malone gloomily. "We'd better get back to your room."

The lift-man ran them up to the next floor, and they went along to Rushton's sitting-room.

They saw Tony just coming in by the window.

"No use, guv'nor," he reported, "they must have got away. I went clear to the lane at the back, and I saw a big saloon car driving off. I'll bet it belonged to Menes."

"I think Tony is right," agreed Malone. "But you see, Rushton, what it means? You won't get away from Cairo, if they can help it."

Rushton looked savage.

"I'll give them all the chance they want if I can get a crack at their hide-out."

Malone smiled thinly.

"That, my dear fellow, is exactly what you are going to have. I came round here just to offer you that opportunity."

"You mean that?"

"Yes."

"When do we go into action?"

"To-night, and you can have as many men as you wish."

"Then I'm your man, Malone. I'll dig out some of those vipers, or you can ship me back in a wooden box."

And at that same moment Prince Menes was in a huddle on the same matter.

CHAPTER 18.

Prince Menes was in a savage temper, although nothing of this was revealed in the suave countenance he turned to those who were grouped about the large, oval table, in a cool, ground floor room in his great palace.

It was a remarkable gathering to take place almost openly in a storm centre such as Cairo.

On Menes' right, indicating his importance in Menes' scheme of things was Wu Ling, also prince in his own right, and in his own country far greater power and prestige than Menes was in Egypt. And, despite the difference in race and creed, there was some strange affinity between those two men, both of such ancient civilisations.

Brady was on Menes' left. His position was by no means as important as that of Mathew Cardolak, who had been acting as Menes' banker, but, with his usual indifference to the opinions of others, he had coolly appropriated a place next to Menes. After all as Sakr-el-Droog—Hawk of the Peak—he wielded a considerable amount of influence in the Arab world.

Mathew Cardolak was almost opposite Menes at the oval table. The Three Musketeers sat close to him, Madame Goupolis was next to one of those young men, and the Black Eagle sat morosely sullen beside Brady.

It was amazing how Menes had collected them all in little more than a week from the debacle caused by Grant Rushton.

From an Arab village by the sea where Mathew Cardolak and the Three Musketeers had been in hiding since their rescue from gaol and from other places, he had brought them together once more.

Menes knew that, if he were to save what remained of the situation, he must act swiftly and firmly. He was in far too deep himself to stop now. His vast properties were mortgaged to the hilt. Powerful Egyptian circles which were against the Government had supplied him liberally with money in the past, but now they were looking for results—demanding them—and repayment.

If Menes ever did come to power he would have a pretty bill to foot. It would need a very large amount of new taxes—which the unhappy fellaheen would foot—to satisfy the rapacious claims he must meet.

For the moment, he was almost stripped of ready cash, and to ease the position here he was still counting on Mathew Cardolak.

Therefore, it was to him, almost more than to Wu Ling that he deferred.

He reviewed the situation briefly. He made no attempt to find excuses. On the contrary, he put the blame again and again on Grant Rushton. He had a purpose in doing so. He wanted to rouse them all to as deep a hatred of Rushton as he felt himself. He had no need, however, to stress the point with Brady and the Black Eagle.

"It is no use saying now that there has been a leak," he told them, when he thought they were in the right state of mind. "I shall discover that leakage, and when I do I shall know how to put a stopper upon it. But we must face the fact that, through this leakage, information reached Malone Effendi who in turn passed it on to the British Government. Just how or why Grant Rushton was brought into the affair is a matter of no importance. We can guess, however, that he would have been influenced strongly by the knowledge that some of his old friends were involved."

Brady made a noise that sounded like a snort, and he and the Black Eagle looked at each other significantly. The Goupolis did not look up. She was very subdued just now in the presence of Menes.

Wu Ling sat just like a yellow idol. His mask-like face hadn't revealed the slightest expression since he sat down, and his lids, almost closed over the oblique eyes, made only narrow slits over the sloe-coloured pupils.

Mathew Cardolak seemed almost asleep. He had been very quiet since the attack on his yacht. It was a reserve that Menes did not like. If Cardolak were fed up and thinking about cutting his losses, then it would be impossible to go on. It was to Cardolak that he spoke next.

"For the indignity you, Monsieur Cardolak, have suffered, a heavy price will be exacted. Moreover, I have sent to my fort in an oasis in the desert commanding the presence of a very learned priest who possesses the secrets of the ancient priesthood. At his skilled hands you will soon receive new health and vigour. But what will interest you even more is news that I received only this morning. It is to the effect that my own secret investigators have discovered a tomb that they believe will surpass in treasure anything that has ever been found. Immediately this matter is finished I propose putting many men to work to unseal it. It will be your own especial concession and all that is found within it shall be yours."

This was not altogether fiction on Menes' part, for he had been keeping this card up his sleeve for some time.

It had originally been his intention to spring this after he had come to power in order to prise another large donation out of Cardolak, but he knew that he must not dangle a rich lure if he were to hold the eccentric old man.

He certainly succeeded in catching Cardolak's interest, for his interest quickened so that he sat up and looked straight at Menes.

"This is correct, Prince?" he demanded.

"I had confirmation only this morning. It is impossible, however, to proceed with that until matters are settled here."

"What do you expect to do here now when the lid has blown off everything?" growled Brady.

Menes stabbed him with a look.

"Did the lid blow off, as you put it, to such an extent that I was not able to outwit those dogs at the critical moment?"

"No one could have done what his Excellency did," broke in Madame Goupolis, anxious to keep in favour with Menes.

"You certainly sprang a nice little rescue all round," drawled Archie Pherison, who had taken his cue from Cardolak.

"Well, let's hear the rest," said the Black Eagle. "While we talk here that bird Rushton is running around loose. We won't get anywhere until we eliminate him."

"Quite so," agreed Menes, smoothly, "I took immediate steps to ensure his—er—absence from further participation in our affairs. Indeed, possibly at this very moment he has ceased to function."

"I believe that when I see it," muttered the Black Eagle.

"Things should now proceed without a hitch," went on Menes, still talking at Cardolak. "I have arranged for a small submarine to carry out our orders. It will accomplish what the yacht failed to do, but those who control the craft insist upon heavy payment for their services."

Mathew Cardolak intervened quickly.

"Of what nationality is this submarine?"

"Of none. It is a free lance. Those who man it are ready to work for any master providing their demand for payment is met. As soon as they carry out our orders they will vanish from the Mediterranean."

"How much do they demand?"

Menes hesitated for a moment.

He was going to name a large sum and he didn't know just how strongly he held Cardolak's fresh interest.

"One hundred thousand pounds in cash."

Brady laughed grimly.

"I'd blow up the canal and the Residency for that," he sneered.

"Why haven't you done so then?" asked the Goupolis.

Brady swung round upon her angrily, but was arrested by a movement from an unexpected quarter.

It was Wu Ling who caught the attention of the whole table by thrusting a hand inside his silk tunic and bringing out a packet which he flung on the table. "There is a trifle," he said tonelessly. "I believe my servant informed me the packet contains fifty thousand pounds. If there is none forthcoming from any other source I shall give orders for another to be supplied. It is nothing. But what is something is the necessity to complete the matter about the canal,"

At this welcome intervention from such an unexpected source, Menes' black eyes glittered. And, as though to show that he was not to be beaten by Wu Ling, Mathew Cardolak tapped sharply on the table.

"You may count on me for another fifty thousand," he said. "I shall give orders for the sum to be drawn at the bank to-day. But one thing I feel strongly should be done, this time without fail."

"Anything you wish done will be carried out," promised Menes.

"I hope there will be no mistake. It is what you have already mentioned—the elimination of Grant Rushton."

"That will be certain. Indeed, at any moment now I am expecting word that it has been done."

As though in echo of his promise there came a knock at the door.

Since Menes had given orders that he was not to be disturbed under any circumstances except for one purpose, he did not hesitate to call permission to enter.

All eyes turned towards the door as it opened to admit Menes' secretary. There was no telling from that impassive face whether his news was good or bad. He bowed low and approached his master, to whom he whispered confidentially.

But those at the table had little difficulty in guessing that the news he brought was far from Menes' liking, for, as he grasped its import, he gave vent to an oath so violent that even the hard-boiled Brady looked shocked.

CHAPTER 19.

Immediately following that oath commotion sounded outside the door.

Menes' eyes flashed with anger. Here was something unheard of. Who could dare to create such disturbance so close to his august presence?

He snapped an order to the secretary who was cringing in terror, for he could not explain.

There was no opportunity for him to do so had he been able. There was an urgent hammering at the door, which was thrown open to reveal a big, elderly Egyptian in a state of extreme agitation. He seemed oblivious to all but Menes.

"Excellency! Excellency!" he gasped. "I must see you at once. All is discovered."

Menes controlled his anger. This individual was no underling whom he could handle like a dog, but a very high official in the Government who had been acting as his spy there. As one of the most trusted officials he had access to the secret files which contained so much of value to Menes, but now it was very apparent that something had come badly unstuck.

Menes was alarmed lest his news, whatever it might be, would frighten off Wu Ling and Cardolak, and that they would withdraw the fresh aid they had promised.

So, mustering a smiling excuse, he hustled the newcomer into an adjoining room. There he was able to give greater vent to his anger.

"Now then, imbecile, what do you mean by bursting in upon me in such fashion? You will cost me millions of pounds by such madness. Speak—what is it?"

"Excellency, your pardon, but I am ruined— we are all ruined. It is Malone Effendi."

"Speak calmly and to the point," snarled Menes. "My patience is nearing an end. Quick—tell me all."

"Excellency, it is as I said. Malone Effendi. He came to my office this morning and took several files. Before he left he placed seals on all the other files and left one of his armed men on guard."

"You permitted this without protest?"

"Oh, no, Excellency. I protested, but the grinning dog showed me a permit from the Minister of the Interior signed with his own hand."

"So, Fedri Pasha did that, did he?" said Menes softly, "go on.

What then?"

"About an hour afterwards I began to receive messages from my different agents. It seems that Malone Effendi went to the hotel where Grant Rushton is staying. According to your orders I had sent the men to deal with Rushton Effendi. Malone learned of that from the files, but how he could have read my cypher notes I don't know."

"Fool. Fool. Fool," stormed Menes. "You leave such secret papers in your office files?"

"But Excellency, how was I to know that Malone Effendi would take such steps."

"Not to know after all that has happened this week, and after my warning. You are worse than imbecile. The rest—quickly."

"Only an hour ago I was warned that I was to be arrested, I fled to my house, Excellency, but found it unsafe. Then I came here. Excellency, I am ruined. All my estate will be confiscated—"

Menes lifted his hand and struck the other across the face.

"Stop."

His voice was no more than a hiss.

"You come here with such talk as that. Your estates. Your safety. Your arrest. And when you are in danger you go to your own house instead of coming to me. Traitor, do you think that I will forgive this?"

The man was cringing in terror.

In his frantic care for his own safety he had forgotten his position with regard to Menes.

"B-but Excellency—"

Menes struck him again, a measured blow that was not heavy but terrible in its portent.

Then he stepped to some curtains and drew them aside. A panel was revealed. He tapped lightly on this which slid back almost noiselessly to reveal a huge, half-naked Nubian on the other side.

He was armed with a scimitar such as a harem guard would carry, and, indeed, this fellow had been promoted from that service.

Menes spoke a few curt words.

The Nubian stepped through the opening, advancing upon the terrified man, who knew only too well what was coming.

Menes did not even glance at him again.

He waited until the Nubian's huge hands had closed upon the other's throat and he dragged him through the panel, then he returned to the gathering in the next room.

There was nothing in his suavity of manner to indicate the brief drama that had just been enacted so close at hand.

But he knew some explanation was necessary.

"It is well that we have agreed what is to be done," he was beginning when for the third time he was subjected to violent interruption.

This time it came in a form which could not be dealt with so summarily as before.

The door was flung back and a man staggered through.

One hand was clutching at his side in a vain effort to staunch the blood that was being pumped from a deep wound in his side. His eyes were fixed upon Menes, and it was sheer will power that drove the stricken man to speak.

"Excellency," he gasped, "they come—police and soldiers!"

On the last word he pitched forward at Menes' feet. Menes did not attempt to question him. He knew the fellow would never speak again.

But he had no need.

Now, those in the room could hear the distant sound of shots and the shouts and clashing of some growing uproar.

Prince Menes stood thinking. He had need to do so, and quickly, for he needed no telling that someone had got through to the very highest officers in the Government to stage a raid like this.

He was desperate. With everything almost in his grasp he must turn and face this new danger. He could not conceal from the others what was happening. They would know well enough. And that knowledge meant that Cardolak and Wu Ling at least would do anything to save their own skins. The Goupolis was negligible in a situation of this kind. He could not count on Brady and the Black Eagle. The Three Musketeers would go with Cardolak.

His harassed gaze saw the bundle of banknotes still lying on the table where Wu Ling had thrown them. They, at least, meant the sinews he would need if he were to escape from this crisis.

He moved swiftly to the table, but Brady saw his purpose, and with a lightning movement he grabbed the money.

The Black Eagle saw Brady on his feet, the money in his hand. He kicked back his chair and came up, gun in his hand. Prince Menes was standing as though listening. He was paying no more attention to

Brady. He was entirely concentrated on the growing uproar that seemed to be coming nearer and nearer to them.

Wu Ling hadn't stirred a finger. Nor had Mathew Cardolak. It looked as though Cardolak had decided to take his cue from Wu Ling, and the Three Musketeers also remained seated.

Suddenly Menes caught Brady by the arm.

"What are you going to do?" he hissed.

Brady's teeth were showing very white against his black, forked beard.

"I'm getting out of here if I have to shoot my way out," he said curtly. "I don't know whether this is a trap of yours or not, Menes. If it is, you and I will have a settlement later. But no more Cairo gaols for me. What about you, Stone?"

The Black Eagle nodded.

"I'm with you." Then he looked at Menes. "What is all that hullabaloo? Is it that bird, Rushton?"

"What else?" snarled Menes. Then his voice changed as he turned pleadingly to Wu Ling and Cardolak. "I give you my word of honour I do not know who is creating this trouble outside, but my guards will take care of it. There is nothing to worry about. I shall go personally and settle this affair, then I shall return and we can complete matters."

Still Wu Ling sat impassively, and for the second time Cardolak seemed to have gone asleep.

Menes strode to the door and threw it open. The racket outside rose to a startling pitch, and those within the room could hear the sound of guns very close.

It was muffled again as Menes closed the door, but rose to a terrific pitch when Brady jerked open the door to listen. He slammed it quickly, and looked at the Black Eagle.

"We'll never get through that way. The passage is packed. Shall we try the other door?"

"You will remain here, my honourable friend."

It was Wu Ling who spoke, though he hadn't turned his head.

Something in that cold, quiet voice arrested both Brady and the Black Eagle. Brady then gave a blustering laugh.

"If you want to be goofy and stay here, that's your funeral," he blustered. "Me—I'm beating it while the going is good."

Wu Ling came to his feet as though a spring had lifted him. His stiff silk tunic rustled as he glided across the floor and faced Brady and the Black Eagle. In his hand they saw a small silver box.

"You have heard of the Yellow Beetle," he said suavely. "It would be unthinkable that the unworthy head of the illustrious order of the Yellow Beetle should travel abroad without the protection of the sacred beetle. One slight pressure of my finger and a score of the sacred beetles will be released. But it must be certain that they will find honourable mark, so this unworthy one will arrange."

With that he raised his other hand, and before Brady or the Black Eagle could spring aside, a thin stream of spray struck each on the chest. Immediately a strong, not unpleasant odour spread about them, and Brady, at least, knew that nothing he could do would dispel it.

Some hours must elapse before it would vanish through its own slow evaporation. And Brady knew, too, that, once those devilish yellow beetles were released, they would fly straight for the spot where the odour came, a lure they could not resist. He had seen with his own eyes the swift death that followed when the creature thrust its needlelike proboscis into human flesh.

He paled under his mahogany skin. The Black Eagle had heard about the Yellow Beetle, but had never witnessed its effect. He was rather scornful of any sort of mumbo-jumbo, and, with an oath, he would have put Wu Ling aside. But Brady caught his arm.

"Don't be a fool!" he rasped. "Better to risk a bullet than that."

The Black Eagle wouldn't have believed it, but in that moment Brady had saved his life.

Then Wu Ling's voice came again, as quietly impersonal as ever.

"The money, please, honourable friend."

Brady cursed him, but he handed over the packet, and then Wu Ling returned to his chair, where he sat fanning himself as unconcernedly as though he were in the security of his own house in China.

Outside, the uproar reached such a pitch that it could no longer be denied.

CHAPTER 20.

Not even Malone had anticipated such a fierce resistance as was encountered at Menes' palace.

He had a profound knowledge of Egypt, and knew, of course, that the rich nobles (of whom Menes was one) wielded a power and enjoyed an immunity greater even than the barons of feudal England.

Proof of that had come when a complete farce had been the result of the capture of some of those implicated in the great canal plot and the escape of others. Nonetheless, the power of the nobles has been curtailed greatly in the recent constitution of Egypt, and he had scarcely believed that even Menes, most daring and truculent of all the nobles, and through his priestly position the most influential private individual in Egypt, would flout the Government by an open show of arms.

But that was just what Menes was doing.

He knew from the moment news reached him of the failure to assassinate Rushton that something serious would break. It may be that he did not think that it would follow so swiftly, but when he heard the sounds of shots in the courtyard of the palace he had no need to ask the reason. He did not believe, however, that Grant Rushton and Malone would be leading the attack in person.

By the time Menes himself appeared the fighting had spread to the main wing where he had received his guests.

Until he was actual witness of the melee that was in progress, he did not have serious fears of his own position.

But realisation came swiftly enough when, from a narrow "archers" window he looked down upon the struggling mass.

His men had driven the first rush of attackers back along the passage, but they were now coming in from a short corridor that connected with Menes' private apartments.

Menes was no physical coward, but it had never been necessary for him to lift his hand in personal combat. There had always been plenty of guards to do that for him. And he knew now that it was unlikely that personal violence would be offered to him by the Egyptian police or soldiers.

Grant Rushton and Lawrence Malone were a different proposition, however, and as he caught sight of the pair in the courtyard, with Tony beside them, all the savage hatred he felt for these "British Dogs" welled up, so that he had a feeling of violent strangulation in his throat.

He took out an automatic pistol and thrust his arm through the narrow slit of a window.

Beneath, Rushton, Malone and Tony were so occupied with the stress of the fight that they did not know that Menes himself was watching from just above.

Yet some clairvoyant sense must have warned Rushton, for his gaze was drawn upwards, and he saw Menes just about to shoot.

At that exact moment Rushton was in the act of throwing his gun upwards to shoot at a guard who was leaping over the body of a man he had just shot down.

Instead of pressing the trigger as intended, Rushton carried the gun higher, then his finger dragged back in a snap shot at Menes.

Both guns seemed to speak on the same instant.

Without the opportunity of taking careful aim, Menes would have been a poor shot at any time. On this occasion, had nothing intervened, it is probable that his bullet would have struck Rushton in or very close to the heart.

But just on the point of pulling the trigger he saw that Rushton had discovered him, saw Rushton's arm jerk up, and knew he was going to shoot.

It served to disconcert him at the critical moment, and when something struck his arm, jerking the gun from his grasp with paralysing violence, he did not need to see Rushton still on his feet to know he had missed.

Menes sprang back out of view.

Rushton shouted to Malone and Tony.

They saw Rushton leaping over a couple of prone forms and making for the entrance to the building.

They had missed the lightning exchange between Rushton and Menes, but knew that some new factor had sent Rushton charging in that fashion.

They followed.

Rushton vanished through the doorway, and half a dozen of Malone's own police officers followed.

Malone and Tony gained the passage inside just in time to see Rushton shooting from behind a pillar at a bunch of Menes' guards. Then Menes appeared at the top of a short flight of stairs.

He was gesticulating violently, and apparently shouting

something, but on account of the uproar they could hear nothing of what he was saying.

Rushton made such a savage rush for the bottom of the stairs that he drove a way clean through the packed guards.

Tony, seeing the achievement, was amazed. Rarely had he seen Rushton so determined to reach his man. He followed, but the guards closed in again, separating him from Rushton. Then two hefty fellows overwhelmed Tony suddenly, and he went down, guarding his head as far as possible against the hail of blows that descended.

Malone had seen Tony go down and was in upon the pack like a fury. His gun was going hard, and Tony was flattened by the weight of bodies that fell upon him. Then Malone dragged him out and they charged together for the stairs.

They could see nothing now of either Rushton or Menes, but at the top they saw Menes in full flight with Rushton at his heels.

At this moment a door at the far end flew open and Flash Brady appeared with the Black Eagle close on his heels.

Their guns began crashing on the first throw. There was no pause for questions on the part of this hard-boiled pair. They were out to kill, and quickly, and their intention was by no means softened at the sight of Grant Rushton.

The uproar in that confined space was appalling. The fumes of cordite were bitterly pungent. Menes, between two lines of fire, was in dire peril. It was half a dozen miracles that he escaped.

But escape he did, and in a way that was so astonishing to those others in the passage that fire ceased for a moment.

One moment Menes was flattening himself against the wall as though to escape the stream of bullets, the next he was gone—just like that.

It was as though he had never been there so utterly complete was his vanishing. It was obvious to Rushton that he had gone by way of some secret panel in the wall, but in the face of the attack which Brady and the Black Eagle were pressing there was no time now to investigate the mystery.

Then another startling thing happened.

For the first time, Brady seemed to have caught sight of the press of men farther along the corridor with Malone and Tony at their head. Brady was too coldly methodical to throw his own life away unless he were caught like a rat in a trap. It had been as much to settle accounts with Menes as anything else that had brought him out of the room again, but now, with a quick word to the Black Eagle, he dashed back, carrying the Black Eagle with him.

The door slammed just before Rushton reached it, and by the time he got it open, he was met with a sight so different from what he had expected, he stood in sheer astonishment.

None of the others had risen from the table. There was Wu Ling, fanning himself as quietly as though no such thing as a racketing automatic existed.

Opposite him was Mathew Cardolak, seemingly half-asleep. He was a wily old bird was Cardolak. And, smoking unconcernedly, were the Three Musketeers. Madame Goupolis was not to be seen. In fact, she had vanished some time since. Brady and the Black Eagle were also gone.

Malone and Tony joined Rushton. Malone gave a low whistle, then he turned as his own officers, now carrying everything before them, reached the door.

"Wait," he ordered, then he looked at Rushton quizzically.

"Well, can you explain it?"

"I think so," was Rushton's slow answer. "And I don't see what we can do. After all, they haven't lifted a hand in resistance."

"And I'm hanged if my authority covers this. We'll have to get after Menes and the others. They resisted all right."

"If they're not already too far away," finished Rushton drily. "I fancy Menes will have many secret passages by which he can escape, and I doubt if your authority would run to a search of the whole place."

"No, and nothing like it."

Malone swore.

He was looking at the silent group about the table.

They had, of course, heard every word that passed between him and Rushton, but still betrayed not the slightest sign of awareness of their presence in the room.

"I'm hanged if I don't feel like hauling them in and taking a chance," muttered Malone, so furious was he at this cool defiance.

As though he had just finished communing with himself Wu Ling stopped his fanning, and with a click, the fan closed and vanished in the sleeve of his tunic.

Then he rose, and placing both hands across his abdomen, bowed ceremoniously to the others at the table.

Cardolak opened his eyes and gave a brief response.

The Three Musketeers rose and bowed from the waist as one man.

Wu Ling turned and started for the door. He gave not the slightest sign that he recognised Rushton and Tony.

He gave another impersonal bow, and not a hand was lifted to stay him. Indeed, as the dignified figure passed down the corridor, Rushton smiled at the grim humour of it all.

"Well, that's that," he murmured, "I think we'd better let the others follow him, Malone. I'm going to hunt Menes and the others. I leave it to you to deal with this bunch as you see fit."

But Rushton shook his head. "There isn't a confounded thing I can do unless they show force of arms. They have been released or are officially missing. Menes is the key and is a key we won't find easily."

Then he lifted his voice. "Okay my slick fellows, you are free to go if you wish. But you'd better make the most of your opportunity, because I might change my mind and take a chance."

Then he turned away. He was too wise a bird to waste time darting at shadows.

He was right, too, about Menes.

The next he heard of him was a rumour that he was entrenched in force at his fort in a distant oasis in the Libyan desert, and Madame Goupolis with him. It was a criminal combination that would be functioning again, and Rushton hoped devotedly that, if he came up against it again, his hands would be free from red tape.

THE END.

[55000 WORDS]

www.ingramcontent.com/pod-product-compliance
Lightning Source LLC
Chambersburg PA
CBHW050824180626
46814CB00004B/1440